DRIVING
THE
BUGMOBILE

DRIVING

THE

BUGMOBILE

ALAN ORLOFF

To my mother, who tried to teach me how to swim every summer. (I finally learned, forty years later!)

Praise for Driving the Bugmobile

"*Driving the Bugmobile* is an emotional coming-of-age story that highlights the pain of growing up and not knowing if the person you're becoming is who you want to be, and deciding who deserves to come along for the ride. I absolutely loved it!"—Melanie Hooyenga, author of the YA psychological suspense *The Quiet Unraveling of Eve Ellaway*.

"Take a ride with Alan Orloff's *Driving the Bugmobile*, a winning coming-of-age novel about Nick Carlin, who's navigating the bumps in the road through his teen years. From first crushes, to new sketchy possible stepfathers, to dealing with the loss of a parent, you'll laugh, you'll cry, but you won't be able to put it down until its stellar characters reach the end of their journeys!"—Lee Matthew Goldberg, acclaimed author of *The Mentor* and *The Great Gimmelmans*.

Chapter One: T-minus 15 days

Summer 2016

Sometimes a Pool Noodle is Just a Pool Noodle

I could do this. I *had* to do this.

Stroke, stroke, stroke. Blow bubbles out through my nose. Kick, kick, kick. Turn my head and breathe through my mouth. My swimming mantra. I repeated it over and over.

I took a deep breath, counted silently to three, then pushed off the wall, aiming for the deep end of the pool. Face underwater, I set my arms in motion, extended my legs, and began kicking.

"Let's go. Pull, pull, pull," Dante yelled as he walked along the side of the pool, pacing me. "Kick. Kick. Kick."

I pulled. I kicked.

"Kick faster, *faster.*"

I cranked up the speed of my legs, kicking as hard as I could. Behind me, the water churned. If I kicked any harder, my feet would fly off.

"Now, breathe!"

I turned my head to take a breath, and about a gallon of putrid pool water rushed into my mouth. I stood and spit out the water, gasping for breath.

"Shit!" Dante jumped into the pool, grabbed my arm, and walked me over to the wall. "Did you forget to blow bubbles, Carlin?"

"I was trying to—"

"Don't try. Do." He stared at me for an extra beat. "Let's go back to the drills. Grab onto the side of the pool and kick while you practice blowing bubbles."

I grabbed the side of the pool, sucked in a lungful of air, then lowered my head into the water, squeezing my eyelids shut even though I wore goggles. I extended my legs and kicked but couldn't bring myself to blow out any air. I was afraid if I tried, water would rush up my nose.

"I don't see any air bubbles. Blow out." He raised his voice to be heard over the splashing. "Blow!"

I held my breath a moment longer, then tried to exhale but somehow water got up my nose. Somehow, water *always* got up my nose. I stopped kicking, and my legs slowly sank to the bottom. I stood in the pool, coughing and spluttering.

"Jesus, not again," Dante barked as his head tilted skyward. "My little sister can swim better than you. And she's four!"

That disgusting chlorine smell and taste up my nose made me want to puke. But I needed to learn how to swim, and if getting blitzed by pool chemicals was part of the process, then I'd deal with it. What I didn't want to deal with was getting shouted at by that asswipe Dante Tanner.

"Maybe we should—"

"Shut up and listen, dude. All you have to do is blow the air out. Gently. Through your nose. Then you turn your head and take another breath. Through your mouth. Then you repeat. Over and over. Breathe in, blow out. Breathe in, blow out. Simple. Like this." He demonstrated taking a breath, then rotating his head, then blowing out. I'd seen him demonstrate the proper way to do it twenty times a day, three days a week, since the end of July. I knew what I was supposed to do, I just couldn't do it. When it came to swimming, I was a total reject.

He fixed his gaze on me—at least I thought he did. His ever-present mirror shades made it hard to see exactly *what* he was looking at. How he managed to keep them on while he taught me was a mystery. "You need to learn how to breathe in the water. Otherwise, you're never going to learn how to swim. That what you want?"

I shook my head, but I recognized futility when I saw it. Swimming came easy for most people. Like Dante. He was only a year older, a senior at Chantilly West High. But he towered over me by about six inches and outweighed my scrawny ass by fifty pounds. He always seemed to have a five o'clock shadow, even at ten in the morning. I shaved once a month, whether I needed to or not.

Dante was a lifeguard and could swim like a piranha; I swam like a bowling ball. An uncoordinated one. Hence the lessons.

"You got asthma?" he asked.

"Nope."

"Tuberculosis?"

"Nope."

"Missing a lung?"

I shook my head. I didn't *think* I was missing a lung.

"Well, something's going on. You got no wind. You smoke, right? That's the problem here." He nodded, as if he'd solved the Riddle of the Sphinx. "Pack a day?"

"I don't smoke."

"Come on, sneak a few behind the barn now and then?"

There wasn't a barn within ten miles of where we lived. "Nope. Never smoked."

"Not even weed?"

I shook my head. Dante was on the varsity football team. He could bench press me if he wanted. He could probably swim with his hands tied behind his back while smoking a fat cigar and wearing shades. Didn't matter. He was a stuck-up jock. A stuck-up *jerk*. "No. Nothing. I don't smoke anything."

He sneered, and his face said he didn't really believe me but was tired of asking. "Uh-huh. Smoking will kill you. But shit, my grandma can hold more air than you. You sure you're not handicapped or something?"

If I didn't need to learn how to swim—absolutely *need* to—I would have walked out right then. And if I had more guts—and muscles—I might have kicked him in the nuts first. But some things, no matter how painful, had to be endured. "No. I'm not handicapped. I just don't know how to swim."

"At this rate, you may never learn." Dante shot a glance at the large clock hanging over the pool office. "Time's up. See you on Monday. Of course, there's no harm in admitting defeat. Not everyone is cut out to swim." He braced his muscle-bound arms on the side of the pool and hoisted himself out of the water, then strode off without another word.

Like I said: *asswipe*.

Above me, a string of blue and white banners fluttered in the breeze. On the pool deck, rows of vinyl-webbed chairs with short legs faced the water. Off to the side, a white tent had been erected next to the baby pool, offering shade to sensitive-skinned tots.

I draped my arms over the edge and watched two lifeguards gather up a few wayward towels and goggles. The pool had just opened for the day, and the energy level was about to rise, fueled by people looking to escape the heat and humidity. By three o'clock, the temperature would be unbearable, and most of the neighborhood would flock to the pool, looking for relief. If not for my mother's ultimatum, you wouldn't find me here. No thanks. I'd stick to dry land and air-conditioning.

The activity level at the pool had been even more frenetic earlier.

Swim team began at the crack of dawn and went until ten. The next hour was lesson time, when the lifeguards could make a few bucks teaching kids to swim. Most of the students were barely out of diapers—then there was me. Sixteen years old and couldn't swim. It wasn't for lack of lessons, either. Since I turned six, my mother had enrolled me every year, at least until I reached puberty. And every year, I'd make a little progress, but never quite put it all together.

This didn't make my mother a happy camper. She'd blame it on the instructors—even though I told her it was me, that I didn't like the water. We kept joining different pools, hoping that being in a new environment with different teachers would help. No luck. Six pools and ten years later, I still couldn't swim.

I climbed out of the pool using the stairs at the shallow end, feeling like I carried lead weights in the pockets of my swim trunks. I retrieved my towel and dried off. People trickled out of the locker room entrances, now that open swim had started. A gaggle of kids, most between the ages of six and thirteen, scrambled for various pool toys: multi-hued noodles, basketballs and volleyballs, floaties and kickboards for the younger ones. Excited shouts and squeals joined the sound of lounge chairs being scraped across the concrete deck as their parents arranged little poolside oases. The smell of coconut sunscreen began to waft through the air. Pretty soon, the calls of "Marco" and "Polo" would contribute to the cacophony, and everyone would be enjoying the summer swimming hole ritual.

Man, did I hate the pool.

* * *

I hung around by the circular driveway waiting for my mom to pick me up. Normally, I walked home, but this morning as I left the house, my mother told me—in no uncertain terms—I was to wait for her after my swim lesson. And that's exactly how she said it. "Nick-o, in no uncertain terms, I want you to wait for me after your swim lesson. I've got something important I need to tell you."

I couldn't imagine what the big news was. If my mother had won the lottery or something, I'm sure I would have heard the screaming. It probably had something to do with her business—she owned the Northern Virginia franchise of Bugs 'B' Gone Pest Control. She'd been saying how busy things had been lately. I guess for us, that was good news, even though an increase in pests and vermin probably wasn't good for society as a whole. Maybe she was going to hire an employee. That would be fine with me; it'd give her someone else to boss around.

On the other hand, the news could be bad. That's what had my nerves on edge all morning.

After a few minutes of standing, I moved to a bench with a little plaque saying it had been made from recycled plastic grocery bags. If I leaned back and looked to my left, I could see the lifeguard behind the check-in counter reading a magazine. She barely glanced at the members' cards as they flashed them. Heck, half of the people didn't even show their cards before entering the locker rooms. I'm not sure how much the pool cared about who belonged and who didn't.

As I waited, I kept alert for anybody who might know me. Getting picked up by your mom wasn't cool. At all. *Especially* in the Bugmobile.

Luckily, my mother arrived before I spotted anyone I knew. She came screeching around the circle, and everyone turned their heads to gawk. She drove an old, bright green PT Cruiser covered with dog-sized pictures of ferocious-looking bugs. Day-glo orange letters above a rabid termite spelled out Bugs 'B' Gone. A rolling advertisement for her pest control business. No matter how many times I saw it—and the car sat in my driveway when it wasn't out infesting the streets—I still cringed.

I ignored the stares and jogged over. "Hey, Mom."

6

She got out and moved around to the passenger side. Ever since I got my learner's permit, I drove us around whenever possible. Practice makes perfect, Mom always said. I jumped in the driver's side and adjusted the mirrors. Slid the seat back. I held my hands out for the keys, but she kept them in her hand.

"Hiya, kiddo. How was the lesson?" She gazed into my eyes expectantly. Always hoping for the best.

"Okay, I guess. I don't think I'm really cut out for swimming, though."

"Just takes some practice. You'll get the hang of it." She kept examining my face.

"Can we get going?" As we sat there in front of the pool, everyone who passed stared at us, no doubt looking for the answer to the burning question: *What kind of crazy people drive a car festooned with hideous pictures of gargantuan bugs?*

"Hold your horses. I've got something I need to tell you."

"Can't you tell me while we're driving?" A guy can only take so many oddball stares. I should have been used to it by now, but some things take longer than others to get over.

"Now, Nick. The more you fuss…"

I sighed. "Go ahead."

"Well, as you know—" Mom's eyes locked onto something behind me, and her head swiveled to my left as she tracked its progress. One eyebrow arched.

I glanced over my shoulder to see what had distracted her and found myself staring right into Allie Merskie's perfect face. She'd graduated in June—headed for Virginia Tech—and I'd heard she was back in town from some extended California vacation. There had even been some talk she'd be working the last half of the summer at the pool. If you counted my hard-up friend Miller's lust-filled wishes as "some talk."

Allie smiled and gave me a little wiggly-fingered wave, then veered off toward the pool's entrance. My gaze followed her as she disappeared into the lifeguard office.

"Who's that?"

I whipped my head around and felt my cheeks getting warm. "Lifeguard. At the pool."

My mom nodded. "Cute."

Poodles were cute; Allie Merskie was hot. "She's okay." I swallowed and waited for my pulse to return to normal.

"So, as I was saying...you sure you're all right?"

"Yeah, I'm fine. It's just...this whole swimming thing. I took lessons when I was little. And now I'm taking more lessons. I still can't swim. Maybe there's something wrong with my bones or something. Maybe I didn't get the buoyancy gene. Let's just say I've given it my best shot and come up short. Don't you always say there's nothing wrong with failing?"

"Swimming's a survival skill. You *need* to know how."

I had been hearing this song for years. "Mom, come on. I don't like the water. I don't even like taking a shower. I'll never go near the water. So why do I have to learn?"

"You'll get the hang of it. Especially now that you've got an incentive." My mom's jaw tightened. "I don't have to remind you about Uncle Steve, do I?"

"No." My throat tightened, and the temperature in the car seemed to rise fifteen degrees in an instant.

"A terrible tragedy," Mom said, oblivious to my impending boil over.

"Mom, can we not talk about—"

"If Steve had been a better swimmer, then things might have turned out differently." I pushed the awful memory from my mind and tried to focus on the present.

"Can we just go now?" I took a deep breath and felt my body slowly return to normal.

She eyed me sideways. "You think Aunt Barrie doesn't wish she *made*

8

him learn how to swim?"

Could adults *make* other adults do things? "I don't even like to fish."

Mom's laser scowl bored into me. "If you don't want to learn how to swim, that's your business. But you won't be getting your driver's license. A deal's a deal. End of discussion."

I growled, just a bit, under my breath. I never wanted to have this discussion in the first place. "Keys, please." I held out my hand.

She reached out and plopped them into my palm. "Well, Nick Carlin, I guess I'll just share my news with you at dinner." She stared out her side window; I started the car. We both sulked in silence as I drove home.

The deal with the devil. I had promised to learn how to swim in exchange for being able to get my driver's license. Of course, it wasn't much of a deal. More like an edict from above. If I didn't pass the swimming test in a couple weeks, I could kiss my high school dating career goodbye. I mean, I'd be relegated to going on double dates with Miller. *If* he ever got *his* license.

I might as well become a Tibetan monk.

Chapter Two

Entering Miller's bedroom was like spelunking in a landfill. Debris—mostly inorganic, I hoped—covered every available surface. Floor, desk, dresser tops. Even his narrow windowsill had junk on it. Upon further inspection, the visible layer seemed to be mostly clothing, as if a laundry blizzard had recently blown through. I shoved aside a stack of *Popular Science* magazines from a chair and sat.

Miller grabbed a handful of underwear from his bed and tossed it on the floor, then belly-flopped onto the mattress. He posed there, like a centerfold in some glossy magazine, a Eurotrash fashionplate in a red t-shirt, orange shorts, and brownish socks. At one point, the socks had been white, but they probably hadn't seen the inside of a washing machine in the past month. Or two. I wondered how much of the clothing strewn about *ever* got washed.

"So what was Allie wearing?" Miller asked.

I'd told him about my mother embarrassing the crap out of me at the pool that morning, and about turning smack dab into Allie's smiling face. "Lifeguard suit. One-piece. Spandex."

"Any nip protrusion?" He put his hands up his shirt and poked his forefingers out from his chest.

"No. I mean, not that I noticed. She was staring at me, in the Bugmobile. I don't think I can go back to the pool after that. I mean, Jesus."

"Come off it. Who doesn't like a car crawling with critters? Or at least bigger-than-life-sized pictures of cockroaches. She probably thinks it's cute. She probably thinks *you're* cute." He wiggled his fingers again, then removed his hands from inside his shirt. "I know I do." He puckered his lips and made smacking noises.

"She probably doesn't even know who I am."

"Actually, you're probably right. Even if she did, dude, you have absolutely no chance with her." Miller hopped off his bed and started pacing in the small room. Each step was accompanied by a crunching noise. "She's two years older than you are. She's going to college. And she's way out of your league." As he spoke, he ticked each point off on his chubby fingers. "In fact, she's so far out of your league, she's playing a different sport altogether."

I picked a flip-flop off the mess on the floor and chucked it at him. It sailed high, hit his lampshade, and bounced to the floor, joining all the other discards of Miller's pitiful life.

Miller stopped pacing and faced me. "Plus, she's probably got a boyfriend." He said it in a high-pitched sing-song.

"Do you know that for a fact? Did Kelly say something?" Kelly was one of Miller's four older sisters, and she'd graduated with Allie. On the surface, having so many sisters seemed like a bad thing, especially when it came down to getting bathroom time. But Miller's sisters had a lot of very hot friends. On balance, I'd say his situation was pretty good.

"Come on. Any girl who looks like her *has* to have a boyfriend. It'd be a crime against nature not to."

"Look, I don't have a thing for her, okay? Let's move on."

Miller smirked. "Okay, sure. She did smile and wave at you, though, right? Maybe I'm wrong, and she has a thing for you. Maybe I'm totally, completely full of shit."

"There's no maybe about it. Now, can we drop it?"

Miller plopped down on the bed, pleased with himself for getting me riled. "How's the swimming going?"

From one sore subject to another. "Just can't seem to get the hang of it."

Miller's eyes went wide. "Dude, you've got to learn how. You can't have your mother driving you around town for the rest of your life. Especially not in the roach coach. It's not that hard. Maybe you need to practice more."

If I didn't learn to swim, I didn't get my license. And if I didn't get my license, I wouldn't be able to chauffeur him around town. As usual, it was all about Miller. "I've been thinking. I don't really need to get my driver's license. I'll just bike everywhere."

Miller's face darkened to a hue approaching eggplant. "No, no, no. You can't give up. Come on. Let's go to the pool now. I'll show you how to swim." He scrambled to his feet and started tugging on my arm.

Hard to admit, but Miller was at home in the water. Maybe flab was extra-buoyant. "Chill. I'm just yanking your chain. I want to learn how to swim. I *need* to learn how to swim. Now let go of me."

He released my arm and exhaled, sending a whiff of tuna fish my way. "Seriously, if there's anything I can do to help, let me know." He sank back down on his bed.

"Thanks. I've still got two weeks to go, and all I have to do is swim the length of the pool and back. Shit, a donkey could do it."

"Donkeys can swim. You can't."

Miller knew all kinds of useless trivia. I picked up the other flip-flop and flung it at him. It ricocheted off his shoulder and landed on his pillow.

"You're awful touchy today." Miller rolled onto his side and propped his head up on one hand. "What's the big news your mother has? Changing your religion? Learning Urdu? You guys moving?"

"Doubt it. Mom's business is here. Her boyfriend's here. I'm in school here. It would make no sense to move."

Miller nodded knowingly. "It's always the thing that makes the least sense. Be sure to write, dude. Winters get lonely in Saskatoon."

"She was pretty excited, whatever it is, so it's probably a good thing. Maybe we're going on a cool vacation."

"I don't know. If she wanted to 'talk to you,' then it's probably a bad thing." Miller threw air-quotes around 'talk to you.' "Otherwise, why didn't she just come out and say it. Like, 'Hey, Nicky, my boy, we're going to Disney World. And I've arranged for a Swedish swimsuit model to be your personal tour guide.'"

The more I thought about it, though, the more I had to agree with Miller. This wasn't going to end well. "What bad thing could it be? I already have to work to get my license."

"Who knows? Don't bust a gut thinking about it. You'll find out soon enough."

"That doesn't make it easier to swallow, my friend."

"Hey, if you are going to Disney World, can I come? And can you see if your Swedish guide has a sister? One who likes to *get busy*?"

"Give it a rest. The last time you *got busy* was never."

Miller saluted me with his middle finger.

I returned the salute and pulled out my phone. Noted the time. Two more hours before dinner. Before Mom's big news. Then I'd know my fate.

Whatever it was, I had a feeling I wasn't going to be *getting busy* either.

Chapter Three

D inner at my house wasn't usually a big deal. Some reheated leftovers, pasta with sauce from a jar, or a couple frozen meals nuked in the microwave. So I knew something was up when I entered the kitchen and saw actual serving dishes on the table. My hopes grew. Maybe Mom's news *was* good, and maybe dinner would be home-cooked for a change.

My hopes were dashed when I noticed a third place set at the table. Then I heard Jason's voice, and my appetite waned.

"Hey, there's the man. How's it going?" Jason asked as he ambled in from the adjacent living room. He'd been going out with my mom for the past year or so. Three weeks ago, he lost his job and had started spending a lot more time around our house. Mom seemed happier, so I guessed it was good, but sometimes he just seemed in the way.

"Okay." I shrugged. "You know, same old stuff."

"Oh, yeah," he said, and I could practically hear the smirk in his voice. "I remember when I was a teenager. Man, the stuff we did." He shook his head.

I didn't have a response, so I settled for my all-purpose shrug. Jason was about five years younger than Mom. And Mom had me when she was seventeen. Which meant Jason was only about twelve years older than I was. He could practically be my older brother, and having your practically-older-brother dating your mom was seriously messed up.

"Where's Mom?" I asked.

"She'll be down in a minute." He walked over to the fridge, retrieved a beer. Popped it open and took a long swig. "She says you can't swim. What's up with that? I mean, can't everyone swim?"

I didn't want to get into it with Jason, so I hit him with another shrug.

"Just need more practice, I guess." He grinned at me, as if he knew exactly what I needed.

Mom bustled into the kitchen. "Hi, honey. Have a good time at Miller's?"

"Yeah, sure."

"Good," she said. "Let's eat."

I helped her put the food on the table, as Jason watched without even offering to lend a hand. Then I took my usual seat, across from my mom, while Jason wedged in between us, on my right.

"I'm famished." Jason patted his considerable gut. "And this looks delicious. Pass the chicken, please."

We passed the food around and everyone dug in, and Mom conspicuously talked about everything *except* her big news. Which must be really bad if she were waiting for dessert to spring it on me.

And wait we did. Jason had to finish his third helping before Mom brought a homemade cherry pie to the table. My favorite. Of course, that meant the news must be terrible.

She took her sweet time cutting each of us a slice. Finally, I couldn't take it anymore. "Mom, what did you want to tell me? You know, your news?"

She looked up from her pie and swallowed. My stomach tightened. Jason was too busy wolfing down his dessert to even notice. "Yes, well." Mom glanced at Jason and cleared her throat. When Jason still didn't come up for air, she reached over and poked him.

He looked at her, then at me, then put his fork down on his plate with a clatter. "Oh, sorry. Great pie."

Mom smiled, but it was a wobbly one, not her usual full-of-teeth grin. "Nick-o, I want to share some big—and happy—news with you." Her smile faltered a tad. She glanced at Jason, who also had a silly grin plastered on his face. "Jason is moving in."

My stomach clenched into a wad the size of a golf ball. Jason, the unemployed slacker, practically my older brother, was moving in? And not like a boarder renting out the basement apartment. He was going to share my mother's bed. On a permanent basis. I felt Mom's chicken and string beans and cherry pie coming back up the way it went down.

I tried to say something, but nothing emerged. Mom stared at me, waiting for some acknowledgment. Approval, a wisecrack, congratulations. Anything. I just sat there with my mouth open. Jason was moving in? This was bad, way bad. Shit, this might even be worse than moving to Saskatoon.

This meant Jason had graduated from being my practically-older-brother, to being my practically-stepfather. Which, it seemed, was only a matter of time.

"May I be excused, please? I don't feel well." And boy, didn't I.

* * *

I stewed in my room, trying to decide if I wanted to text Miller or wait until I could vent to him in person. I kept picking up my phone, then putting it down. What could Miller possibly say to make the situation better? *At least you didn't get your hand caught in the garbage disposal?*

I thought about Jason. Bad jokes, many my mom said were in poor taste. He often reeked of cigarette smoke. I'd heard him arguing with Mom—on more than one occasion—about smoking in the house. Luckily, Mom won that argument. And I got the feeling he had a tough time holding a job. Maybe that's what this was all about. Maybe Jason *needed* a place to stay, at least until he got another job. That thought buoyed my spirit for a few minutes, but when I realized that, although his unemployment might have been what caused him to move in, getting a job probably wouldn't cause him to leave. By then, he'd be too comfortable sponging off us to move out.

There was something else about Jason. I always got the feeling things weren't what they seemed with him. That he was putting on some kind of fake front to the real Jason. A shifty, insincere, rubber mask hiding something repulsive underneath. Like the aliens in *Men in Black*. Was there any truth to my feeling, or was I simply being overly protective of my mother?

Either way, I didn't relish sharing my house—my life—with some outsider.

A soft knock at the door interrupted my pity-fest. "Yeah?"

Mom poked her head in. "Can I come in? I'd like to talk with you."

"Sure." I sat up on my bed, and Mom took a seat next to me.

"Quite a surprise, huh?" she said.

I nodded. Took a deep breath.

"I tried to come up with a good way to break the news, but I didn't know how you'd react."

Badly, that's how. I shrugged.

"I thought about discussing this with you, ahead of time, but…I don't know. Maybe I should have…" Mom trailed off.

If I could have said something to make her apology—or whatever this was—less painful for her, I would have, but I was at a loss. I simply shrugged again.

"Nick-o?"

"Yeah?"

"Are you okay with this? If you're not, I guess we could reconsider, work something else out. I thought…I thought you'd want me to be happy, you know?"

My throat felt tight. "Are you going to marry him?"

She licked her lips. "I don't know, hon. He makes me feel...I care for him a lot, and he cares for me. And I know he thinks you're a great kid, too."

Yeah, right.

"You like him, don't you?"

I sat mum.

"He's never hurt you or anything, has he?" Mom's tone sharpened.

"No, Mom. He's fine." I swallowed. "It's, well..." I knew what I felt but couldn't get the words out. I felt tears coming on.

"I know, hon. It's been just you and me for so long, and now someone else is in the picture. It's only natural to be a little confused. Or angry. Or whatever. Things'll look different tomorrow. Next week. Give this a fair shake, okay? I think you'll get used to it." She patted me on the knee. "What do you say? Will you give it an open-minded try?"

I could tell when my mom really wanted something. "Sure, I'll give it my best. Sure."

She beamed and patted my knee again. "That's my Nick-o. And thanks." She hugged me and kissed my head. With a wink, she got up and headed for the door but stopped and turned before leaving. "Oh, one more thing. I have an urgent job tomorrow morning. A swarm of wasps got inside some poor woman's basement, so I won't be able to go driving with you. But I asked Jason, and he'd be happy to take you out. We wouldn't want to miss Beltway Saturday, would we? I told him you'll be ready at 7:30. Good night, sweetie."

Things just kept getting better and better.

Chapter Four: T-minus 14 days

Let's Get Going

I f you're a driver in the Washington, D.C. area, eventually you'll have to contend with the dreaded Beltway, the highway circling our Nation's Capital. Full of impatient, harried, and often aggressive drivers during off-peak hours, it's a total free-for-all during rush hours. That's why Mom and I—mostly Mom—decided to practice driving during the quiet times and work our way up from there. Weekend mornings were best, so Beltway Saturdays were born.

Every Saturday morning, the earlier the better, we'd hop on I-66 East—also a hotbed of crazy driving and commuter nightmare, according to Mom—and take it to the Beltway. Then, we'd either go north into Maryland, or south toward the Wilson Bridge, and into Maryland on the other side of the District. It didn't make a difference. Beltway drivers were Beltway drivers, no matter which direction they were heading.

Most of the time, I handled the trip fine. Today, though, with Jason riding shotgun, I was a little nervous. For one, I didn't usually perform well when people were watching me—Mom and friends excepted. And, although I was grateful for not having to drive the Bugmobile for a change, I wasn't used to Jason's car. I prayed I wouldn't wreck it. No telling what he might do to me.

I took neighborhood roads to I-66 without a hitch, and when we approached the Beltway, I got in the right-hand lane to head south, toward Alexandria.

"No, my man. Let's go north," Jason said.

"Mom and I went north last week."

"So. She's not with us now, is she? Take the exit going north."

I shrugged. Didn't make much difference to me. I came off the loopy exit ramp and merged into the stream of cars. Traffic seemed heavier than normal, but Jason kept saying how light it was—compared to 4:30 on a Friday afternoon.

"Okay, let's practice changing lanes," Jason said, glancing over his shoulder from the passenger seat. "See how quickly you can get all the way over to the left."

I was in the second lane from the right, where Mom usually made me stay. She preferred staying clear of those trying to merge onto the highway, and also far from the "race car maniacs" in the leftmost lane. "All the way over?"

"Yeah. We're practicing lane changing, right? So let's change lanes."

I glanced over and a huge, shit-eating grin smirked at me from his doughy face. What did my mom see in him, anyway? "Okay."

I put my turn signal on, checked the mirrors, and waited for a gap in traffic. When it was clear, I changed lanes. Piece of cake.

"Okay. Good. Now do it again."

I put my signal on and checked traffic behind me. A couple of cars were fast approaching, and behind them, more cars. I flicked off my signal.

"What are you doing? Don't drive like a girl. Change lanes." Jason half-turned in his seat and looked out the back window. "After these two cars, do it."

I checked the gap in my mirror. After those two cars, an 18-wheeler loomed large. "It's not clear."

"It's clear enough. I've been driving a long time. This is a learning experience. You won't always have huge gaps, you know." He spoke fast. Something about driving on the Beltway sped everything up.

The speedometer read sixty-five. I flicked on my signal and glanced in the rearview mirror every few seconds, trying to anticipate all the other drivers' moves. Behind me, there seemed to be a lot of vehicles, and they all seemed to be changing lanes. The truck seemed to be gaining ground.

"Now!" Jason said. "Punch it!"

I hesitated, checking the mirror again. That truck...

"Now, dammit!" I sensed Jason's hand reaching toward the steering wheel. Before he could grab it, I jerked the wheel to my left, then straightened out. A truck horn blared behind us, so close it sounded like the *ba-roooom* came from my pocket.

"Whoo-hooo, you made it," Jason said, whooping. "Now step on it."

Jesus, we almost got flattened, and Jason sounded like he'd just stepped off a rollercoaster. My heart pounded in my throat. Behind me, the truck's horn sounded again. My hands jittered on the wheel.

"Pick up the pace, Nick. Come on, come on." Jason said, irritation creeping into his voice.

I sped up to put some distance between us and the truck. The needle on the speedometer approached eighty.

"Hey, how fast have you ever driven?"

However fast I was going now. Mom kept an eagle eye on my speed when we drove together. I'd goosed it up over seventy a couple times before she reigned me in. "I guess right now."

"Heh, heh." Jason glanced around. "Okay. Coast is clear. You can let it out here."

"Let what out?"

"Get this puppy going. Step on the gas. Come on, you know you want to."

Part of me did want to. Part of me wanted to hit one-hundred and race around the banked oval and go for the checkered flag. But not now, not here. Not with a thousand other cars around and cops on the prowl and deep potholes and…and not with my Mom's asshole boyfriend egging me on. I eased up on the accelerator until we were going about sixty-five. I flipped on my turn signal to change lanes and get out of the left lane. Out of the speed zone. I'd had enough NASCAR for one Beltway Saturday.

"Oh man. Grow a set." Jason laughed. "Hey, does your boyfriend know how to drive?"

A half dozen sharp retorts flitted through my mind, but I bit my tongue. Pissing off Jason didn't seem like a good idea, long-term. I glanced in my mirror and changed lanes, then changed lanes again until I was in the second-to-right lane. My heart was still going almost as fast as the car.

I glanced at Jason, and he appeared to be deep in thought. Finally, he spoke. "Okay, okay. You did the right thing. I was just testing you." He slapped me on the shoulder. "You passed. With flying colors. Tiff will be proud."

I hated it when Jason called my mom Tiff. It didn't sound right. Even Gram used her full name, Tiffany. When he called Mom Tiff, I always pictured Mom arguing with someone, and that someone was usually me. "Maybe we should head home now."

"Naw. I got something I need to do in Rockville. It'll be good practice. You could use it. Now, get in the left lane up ahead, and we'll take 270 North."

I shifted lanes and reached for the radio. Jason stuck his hand up. "Nope. You need to concentrate on the road. No tunes." He pulled out his phone and punched in a few numbers. "Hey, Stazzo. I'll be there in about ten minutes. Maybe fifteen, if we don't get the lead out. Okay.

Sure. Later." He hung up and stuffed the phone back into his jeans.

I guess we were on our way to meet Stazzo.

A few minutes later, we got off 270, and Jason directed me with a few terse *make-a-lefts* and *make-a-rights*. We crossed over Rockville Pike and worked our way through some neighborhoods until we eventually emerged at a run-down industrial park. I followed Jason's instructions to turn in and find a parking spot around back.

There were only a few spaces, and all seemed to have a good view of the twin Dumpsters. I pulled in and cut the engine. "You sure we're in the right place?"

"Yeah, I'm sure. I'll be back in a little while." He cocked his head and smiled. "Don't go anywhere." He got out and started for a small service door next to the closest Dumpster, then changed direction and came around to the driver's side. With his hand, he pantomimed rolling down the window. I hit the switch, but nothing happened. He pointed at the ignition, and I realized I needed to turn the key to get the window to work. I did and rolled the window down.

"Yes?"

"Let's have them."

"What?"

"The keys." He stared at me as if I were planning on ditching him the minute he got inside.

I plucked the keys from the ignition and handed them over. Jason made a big show of putting them in his pocket, even patting his pocket twice when they were safely tucked away. Then he went inside.

I got out to stretch my legs and escape the reek of cigarette smoke that oozed from the car upholstery. As I did, a breeze blew the pungent odor of garlic and fish my way. A strip shopping center backed up to the industrial park, and I spotted the source of the stench—another row of Dumpsters in a little alley on the opposite side of a chain link fence. Some handmade signs in Korean were posted on the large trash

23

cans. From the smell of things, it must be a restaurant. Hell, from the smell of things, it must be a whole shopping center full of restaurants.

A generous helping of trash was scattered on the ground, and an old kitchen chair with a peeling vinyl backrest leaned against a whiskey barrel table. I hoped the inside of the restaurant was a little more inviting.

No telling how long I'd be stranded, so I took my phone out and texted Miller. It was always a guessing game whether Miller had phone privileges on any given day. His parents took away his phone for just about anything they didn't like. Teasing his sisters. Being disrespectful. Blowing off homework. Although, to be fair, Miller did a lot of stuff normal people didn't like. *No reply.*

I thought about texting Johnny Bohnert—Johnny B to everyone except his parents—but he was away at a band camp somewhere in the wilds of Pennsylvania, and he was probably blowing his horn on some football field, rather than waiting around for my text. Either that, or he was off chasing the cute flute player he'd texted me about the other night.

I examined Jason's ride while I waited. An older Ford, it looked like it had more than a few miles on it. A fist-sized indentation adorned the back right fender, and it had undergone at least a couple of paint jobs, judging by the white paint visible through the blue in a particularly nasty scratch above the wheel well. Assorted dings and dents decorated the rest of the body. Inside, the seats were torn, and there was a grotesque, splotchy stain on the back seat. If I didn't know better, I'd say someone spilled an entire bottle of bright red fingernail polish, then wallowed around in it for a while.

Sports car or junker, it didn't matter to me. It was kinda nice to drive around in a car *other* than the Bugmobile. In Mom's critter-cruiser, I always got weird looks, and people would often honk and make faces and all kinds of other shit. I think the unwanted attention embarrassed Mom, too. Once, she mumbled something about renting a car to take me out driving, but nothing ever happened with that. Just as well. I think I'd feel guilty spending money with a perfectly drivable Bugmobile in the driveway. Humiliating, yes, but already paid for.

Jason's clunker Ford didn't really match the guy I thought I knew. He struck me as kind of shallow, someone who'd care a lot about what his ride looked like. I would have thought he'd be driving a sports car. Probably didn't have the money.

He'd been a warehouse manager, but his company got bought out, and it merged with another company, so they didn't need his warehouse anymore. He'd spent the last few weeks of work crating up stuff. Man, that must have sucked, knowing you were helping someone else take over your job.

Since he got laid off, he said he'd been looking for other jobs, but I never saw him in a suit or heard about him going on any interviews. Of course, I tried not to be in his business—who knew where he went during the days.

I stared at the door where he disappeared, willing it to open and disgorge him. What was he doing in there? I glanced around again. I was hidden from anybody in the industrial park, and no one in the shopping center parking lot could see me either, unless they happened to be behind the restaurants in the smelly alley—and right now it was empty. If someone came along and murdered me, who would know? Would Jason find my body and toss it into a Dumpster, rather than have to deal with the hassle of calling the cops and waiting around to answer questions? He seemed like the type who would want to avoid anything that inconvenienced him.

With my phone, I took a few pictures of the surroundings, just in case they found my dismembered body lying around. At least they'd know where I'd been killed. Maybe I'd be lucky and snap a shot of my killer as he approached me with his chainsaw.

Ten minutes went by, then ten more. I was tempted to go knock on the door, but what would that accomplish? He'd just tell me to go back to the car and wait for him.

I settled for checking my Twitter feed.

Ten more minutes went by, then the door banged open and Jason came striding out. "Okay, all done. Let's go."

We both got in and buckled up. He had a brown paper lunch bag on his lap, the top rolled down just like Mom used to do with my lunches in third grade. We came all this way for a PB&J? "What's in the bag?"

He patted it once, then looked at me, eyes narrow. "Nothing."

Anyone else, I probably wouldn't have cared. But the way his face scrunched up and the slight tone of defiance in his voice made me think something was up. Had I just driven Jason to a meeting with his drug dealer? I debated what to do. Drive to the nearest police station? Confront him with my hunch? I swallowed. Maybe it *was* just a sandwich. "Okay. Sure. None of my business."

I slipped the car into reverse and pulled out. Retraced our way out of the industrial park's lot. Turned onto the main road, looking for signs back to 270. I navigated my way through Rockville and back to the highway. Headed south toward Virginia. Cars whizzed by us on both sides, even though I was going more than sixty miles per hour.

Jason stared out the side window, no longer giving me step-by-step instructions. My mind began to wander until a terrible thought hit me, like a crash test dummy slamming into the dashboard. There could be something worse than drugs in that bag.

An engagement ring.

I reached over and popped on the radio, eager for something to take my mind off that depressing scenario, the louder the better.

This time, Jason didn't even say a word.

Chapter Five: T-minus 13 days

What, Me Worry?

The next day, I rolled out of bed around ten and prepared for our weekly Sunday brunch with Gram. She only lived a couple miles away, and we saw her plenty during the week, but she liked having Mom and me over every Sunday morning so she could have something concrete on her schedule—a standing appointment to nag the crap out of us. To be fair, it was mostly Mom she nagged. I was her sole grandchild—she adored me.

I went down to the kitchen to read the Sports section before we left and found Mom standing over the sink, eating a piece of jam-laden toast. She wore her khaki pants and Bugs 'B' Gone green polo shirt, the one with the little smiling cockroach stitched above the pocket. She held up a finger and swallowed, then wiped a few crumbs from the side of her mouth. I knew what she was going to say before she said it.

"Sorry, Nick-o. Got an emergency. And there's no way I'm passing up the weekend surcharge for some of Gram's rock-hard biscuits. You're on your own." Her eyes brightened. "Hey, maybe you can go with Jason. That would be fun. Go wake him if you want to, hon. Gotta run." She snatched a banana from the bunch on her way out.

Me and Jason enjoying some nice scones with Gram? I didn't think so. We'd taken Jason with us once before, about three months ago, and he seemed to get along with Gram—and vice versa. But that was before Jason moved in with us. Who knew what Gram might say—or do—when she found out? I decided to let Jason get some more beauty sleep. I didn't want to get in the middle of some kind of adult tug-of-war. Besides, I could handle Gram on my own.

It only took me about ten minutes to ride my bike to her house, and it felt good to get my muscles moving a little. Ever since I got my learner's permit, I rode my bike a lot less than I used to.

I set the bike down next to the front walk and rang the bell. In a moment, Gram answered, wearing some kind of pink frilly dress and clutching a dust rag in one hand. "Hiya, Nicky. How are you, my dear?" She pinched one of my cheeks. I guessed I was growing up—usually, she pinched both cheeks. Elbowing past me, she peered through the screen door onto her porch. "Where's your mother?"

"She couldn't make it. A big job came up, last minute. She sends her regrets."

Gram's eyes flashed, then she quickly returned to grandmother status. "Well, more food for us, right? Come in, come in." She turned and bustled down the hall. "Why don't we sit and visit a bit before we eat?"

I followed her into a large sunroom in the back, next to the eating part of the eat-in kitchen. "Want something to drink? Some orange juice?" On the coffee table, there was a pitcher of OJ, along with three glasses already filled to the brim with juice.

"Sure. Sounds good." I carefully picked up the closest glass and slurped a bit from the top so it wouldn't spill. It tasted like Gram had squeezed it herself, which wouldn't surprise me.

"Oh, just a minute." She headed back toward the kitchen.

Gram's house was always spotless, and there was never any stuff strewn about. At our house, we practically had clutter down to an art form. I guess there were two kinds of old ladies. Those who had so much time their houses were always spotless, and those who had lost touch with reality and didn't care—or forgot—about cleaning up. Those were also the ones with dozens of cats prowling around.

Although Mom had me when she was only seventeen, Gram had waited until she was in her late thirties before having Mom. So she was somewhere around seventy years old—I could never remember exactly. She didn't always act that old. In fact, except for the whole cleaning thing, she acted pretty young.

Gram returned and set a plate down on the table next to the pitcher of juice—two rows of saltines covered with something greenish. Orange speckles dotted the glop. "Appetizers. I got the recipe from my Judith."

"Uh, thanks. I don't want to ruin my appetite. They look good, though." I didn't know who her Judith was or what she did for a living, but I was pretty sure she wasn't a chef.

Gram picked one up and popped the whole thing into her mouth. Chased it with a sip of juice. "Needs more salt."

I drank some more juice. When I looked up, Gram was staring at me. "I think you've gotten taller since last week."

How could she tell? I was sitting down. Besides, she said that every week. "I don't know. My clothes still fit the same."

She waved her hand at me. "Bah. How can you tell? Everything's so baggy. You could fit someone else in there with you."

It didn't surprise me that Gram was years behind on the fashion trends. "You're right. I've tried it. My teachers don't think it's funny, though."

Another hand wave accompanied by a small smile. "So, how's the driving going?"

"Fine. Good. It's kinda cool."

Gram wrinkled her nose. She didn't drive much anymore, mostly just to the grocery store three blocks away. "Uh-huh. Is your mother a patient teacher?"

29

"She's usually not too bad. You know."

Gram nodded, as if she did. "How's the swimming?"

I shifted on the uncomfortable wicker loveseat. "Getting there. I'm no Michael Phelps or anything, but I haven't drowned yet." As soon as the words came out of my mouth, I knew I'd screwed up. The specter of Uncle Steve appeared, and my hand holding the glass of OJ started trembling. I quickly set it down on the table so it wouldn't slosh over.

I braced for some kind of tearful explosion from Gram. Of course, I had my own demons to contend with. I closed my eyes, summoned happy thoughts, and hoped that Gram hadn't heard me. Or that she didn't associate my comments with Uncle Steve's tragedy.

"Good, good." Luckily, her attention had drifted to the lamp on the side table next to me. She rose slowly, produced the dust rag from somewhere in the folds of her dress, and proceeded to give the brass lamp a good rubdown. "Fingerprints." She moved to the lamp on the other side of the loveseat and began polishing.

Crisis averted. When my hand was steady enough, I picked up my orange juice and took a sip. Stole a glance at the apple-shaped clock on the wall and discovered I'd been there only five minutes. Crap!

"Okay. Sorry about that." Gram returned to her seat and secreted the dust rag back into her dress. "If I didn't take care of those smears now, I'd just forget about them. You understand, right?"

"Sure, Gram. No big deal."

She gave me a big smile. "Anything else new?"

I set my glass down on the coffee table. *You mean, did Mom's boyfriend move in with us?* "Uh, nope. Not that I can think of."

Gram eyed me funny. "I called your house this morning. I wanted to see what kind of jam your mother wanted—she's picky about her jam. Likes grape and strawberry but can't stand raspberry. Too many little thingys that get stuck in her teeth. What, she can't floss? Anyway, I guess you'd left already."

"Any kind of jam is good with me."

Gram nodded and leaned forward on her chair. "When I called, that fella Jason answered. Your mother's friend."

My new roomie. I tensed, and my mind ran through a dozen possible ways this conversation could go. "Oh?"

"Yeah. Seems friendly enough." She tilted her head at me. "What's he do?"

"What do you mean?"

"For a living. What's he do?"

"Uh, I think he's a warehouse manager or something." Currently, he's more of an "or something," but I didn't see the need to go into details.

Gram nodded. "You like him?"

I shrugged. "Yeah. He's okay, I guess. Mom likes him."

"Of course she does. Your mother…" She waved the hand again, as if she were swatting at flies. "Did I already ask if anything else is new?"

I conjured an image of Jason's smirk. Maybe he should have come over, if for no other reason than to appease Gram's curiosity. "Nothing's really new, Gram. Just enjoying my summer. Driving, swimming, hanging out. You know." I took a sip of OJ, making sure to avert my eyes from Judith's saltine creations.

Gram nodded sagely. "You have a girlfriend?"

"Uh, no. Not right now." I knew this line of questioning was coming—it always did. Sometimes before we ate, sometimes during brunch, sometimes as we were saying goodbye at the door. I didn't always know when, but it was inevitable.

"A smart, good-looking boy like you? I bet the girls are very, very disappointed."

"Thanks, Gram. I'll keep my eyes open for a nice girl, okay?" Allie Merskie was a nice girl. I imagined bringing her over for brunch one Sunday, and the look on Gram's face when I answered her girlfriend question with an actual girlfriend in tow. Of course, I didn't want to be responsible for giving Gram a coronary.

"Nick? You okay?" Gram stared at me. "Are you getting enough sleep?"

"Huh? Oh, sure. Sorry. Just spaced out for a second."

"I asked if you were ready to eat."

"Yeah, I'm starving." Just as long as we weren't eating anything her Judith made.

Chapter Six

That afternoon, Miller and I went to the mall. We were hanging out in the cavernous food court, not too far from the entrance to the 12-screen multiplex. Us, and about three hundred other teenagers, drinking, eating, and ogling each other.

As Miller's head swiveled around like a broken wheel on a shopping cart, he kept saying, "*Now.*" Somewhere, he'd read that teenage boys think about sex every five seconds, and he was testing the theory, complete with play-by-play. "How about you? Five seconds seem about right?"

"I don't think you're going to attract any girls when you keep saying 'now.' They'll think you have some kind of weird affliction."

"Whatever. I'm better than your average dude. I think about sex every three seconds. That's probably a good thing, right?"

"Sure. Girls are really impressed by guys mumbling to themselves every few seconds." The mall was pretty crowded. I bet if we stood there long enough, we'd end up seeing twenty or thirty people we knew.

Miller stopped timing his sex drive. "How was your brunch? Did *Gramama* pull out one of her stogies after the meal?"

I'd told him about Gram's new vice—smoking super skinny and super smelly thin cigars. The box said Black and Mild; she called them Black and Wild. "I don't know. I left right after I cleared the table. Told her I had to go cut the grass."

"Watch out. You'll fry if you lie to your grandmother too many times." He slurped from his Coke.

"I wasn't lying. I went home and cut the grass."

"Oh." He nodded to my right. "Incoming."

Zach Worth and his posse swarmed past the Burger King counter, coming our way. Miller and Zach had a habit of arguing about the littlest things, and Miller usually ended up fuming after their *discussions*. I didn't much care for the guy either, but I did my best to let his shit roll off my back.

When Zach spotted us, he veered in our direction. His posse veered too. "Hey, Bugboy. Hey Miller. What's up?"

I nodded and tried to look uninterested, but Miller took the bait. "Not the stock market. What's up with you?"

Zach rolled his eyes. "So, did you pass tenth grade? Or will you go around again? Might be good, you can swing and miss with a whole new set of girls."

Miller's parents were always on his case about his bad grades. It sucked for him that his classmates busted on him about it, too.

"Can't blame a guy for trying," Miller said.

Zach opened his mouth to—presumably—launch another missile at Miller but closed it before blast off. He turned to his buddies. "Come on, let's get out of here before someone spots us talking to these losers." He turned back to us. "Good luck, Miller. You'll need it." He jerked his head, and his crew followed him, toting their bags from Abercrombie and Hollister.

"Assholes," Miller said, although they were no longer within earshot.

"You should do what I do. Ignore them." I raised an eyebrow. "You did pass, didn't you?"

"Yeah, sure." Miller grinned. "Just barely. And boy, was my father pissed. You'd have thought someone cut off his foot or something."

His expression soured. "But..."

"What?"

"They started talking about sending me to a different school. A military school." Miller's face turned pale.

"Which one?"

"Dunno. But the way they were talking, I'm pretty sure I won't like it."

"What are you going to do?" Sending Miller to a military school didn't sound like a good thing. For the school or for Miller.

"I could always run away and join the circus." He tilted his head. "They still have circuses, don't they?"

"Well, you are qualified. The circus always needs a good clown."

Miller dropped the subject, and we drank our sodas for a while, content to check out the river of people as it flowed along the mall concourse.

Miller elbowed me. "Hey, there's your girlfriend." His eyes were much better at spotting people in a crowd than mine were. He called out her name and waved.

I'd known Laura DiBennetti since first grade. We were good friends but never anything more. "For the millionth time, there's nothing between me and Laura. Just friends."

"Yeah, right."

Laura and a cute blonde came over.

"Hi guys," Laura said.

I nodded. "Hey."

"Hey, hey, hey," Miller said.

The two girls set down their bags. "This is my cousin, Amy. She's visiting from North Carolina. A mini-family reunion," Laura said.

"Hello, Amy. Welcome to our world," Miller said, standing up a little straighter. "They have malls like this in North Carolina?" He emphasized the words, *North Carolina,* saying them slowly with an overdone southern accent. If Amy couldn't tell Miller was a weirdo just by looking at him, it was obvious now.

"Uh, sure. We have plenty of malls," Amy said, with just a trace of an accent. She had long straight hair and a killer smile.

"So, doing a little shopping?" I asked.

"We were tired of hanging around the house, listening to our parents drone on about all the hardships of their childhood. So we left," Laura said.

"Oh, it wasn't that bad," Amy said. "We don't get together very often. It's just—"

Miller interrupted. "You know what they say. You can pick your friends, but you can't pick your family." He chuckled quietly. "And you definitely can't pick your friend's nose." He chuckled a little louder.

Both Amy and Laura made faces at me. Amy seemed especially confused. I shrugged and gave them a "what-are-you-going-to-do look." Miller was oblivious, as usual. I'd been waiting years for Miller to mature, but the longer I waited, the less confidence I had that he actually would.

"Yeah, well, you can hang out with us for a while, if you want," I said.

Laura's eyes brightened. "Sure. That'd be—"

Amy put her hand on Laura's arm. "I don't know. We probably should be getting back. Everybody will be wondering where we are." Something unspoken passed between them. If I had to guess, I'd say Miller made Amy uneasy. I didn't blame her.

"Oh, right. You're right. We need to get back. Sorry, Nick," Laura said, looking right past Miller. "Maybe we can hang out another time, huh?"

"Yeah, sure," I said.

Laura picked up her shopping bag, then set it down again. "Hey, how's the swimming going?" she asked.

"Okay." She knew all about my swimming-for-driving deal. In fact, she'd offered to help teach me, but I didn't want her to see how much of a failure I was, so I told her no thanks. "Just a little more practice and I should have it down."

"Good, good. Well, you promised me one of the first solo rides, so I'm counting on that."

Amy grabbed Laura's arm again. "Come on, we should get going. Your mom said she'd pick us up at…" Amy glanced at her watch, "five minutes ago."

Laura and I hugged goodbye, and she gave Miller a quick hug, too. Then Miller tipped his head at Amy. "Nice meeting you. And if I'm ever in North Carolina…" He trailed off.

Amy looked as if she'd just swallowed a live cricket.

"Bye," the girls called out in unison as they headed down the concourse, away from the exit.

Miller spoke first. "Man, she was hot. And I think she wanted me. How far away is North Carolina?"

"Earth to Miller, Earth to Miller. Come in, Miller." I squawked into an imaginary transmitter in my hand. "You have strayed too far into outer space. Please return to reality."

"You don't know squat about stuff like that." He shook his head slowly. "Dude, you are so blind."

I was the blind one?

"And you're so dumb." He kept shaking his head, like a sideways pendulum. "You don't even know that Laura is way into you."

"What?"

"Laura. Your *girlfriend*. I don't know what your problem is. She was practically drooling all over you. You should totally go for it."

"You're so full of shit. I've known her since forever. We're just pals. Trust me."

He poked me in the shoulder. "You should trust *me*. Laura DiBennetti wants you. Bad."

Miller *was* full of shit. As usual.

Chapter Seven: T-minus 12 days

Is It Getting Warm In Here?

I'm six years old. My family is on vacation with Uncle Steve's family at their cabin in the woods. Early one morning, Uncle Steve takes me out to the nearby lake so we can go fishing in his beat-up little rowboat.

We're having a great time when all of a sudden, Uncle Steve stands up, clutches his arm, tries to say something, then topples over into the water as I watch in horror.

I dive into the murky water, find Uncle Steve, and drag him back into the boat. Then I row the boat to shore, to safety. Because of my quick action, he makes a full recovery.

I woke up, heart hammering, t-shirt damp, like every other time I woke up from the same dream.

Except it's not *completely* a dream.

In real life, that exact scene played out, with a different, tragic ending. In real life, I didn't jump into the water to save Uncle Steve. In real life, I screamed as I peered over the side of the boat, waiting for Uncle Steve to surface. I yelled his name until my throat was raw, tears flowing down my face. I watched the glassy surface of that mountain lake for what seemed like forever, praying Uncle Steve would reappear.

He didn't, so I curled up into a ball on the bottom of the boat, crying, until Mom came to my rescue, hours later.

In real life, I remember how devastated Aunt Barrie had been after the emergency divers pulled Uncle Steve's lifeless body out of the lake later that day.

Every time I had that dream, I felt out of sorts for quite some time. When I first started having them, I told Mom, and she always said not to worry about it, that it didn't mean anything, just my subconscious blowing off steam, but she always had a tear in her eye when she said it.

After a while, I stopped telling her when I had the bad dreams.

Sometimes it would take days for me to get over one. Reliving the tragedy, wondering what I could have done. Despite Uncle Steve's heart attack, Aunt Barrie always believed that if he were a stronger swimmer, he would have been able to make it back to the boat. She'd passed along that theory to my mother—hence her insistence on making me learn how to swim. And it's not that I don't think swimming isn't important, but I'd given it a damn good try. I just didn't have it in me.

About four or five years ago, I'd mentioned to Mom that sometimes I felt guilty for not jumping in to try to save Uncle Steve. She'd smothered me in a big hug and told me that there was nothing I could have done, I was just a kid. She repeated it about twenty times, and each time she did, she squeezed a little harder.

I told her I believed her.

But to this day, I'm not sure I did. I mean, maybe if I did know how to swim then I could have...

I've tried to forget what happened; I can't. The images of that terrible day are burned into my memory. In the years after the accident, I'd gone to a therapist, Dr. Williams, and she'd helped me process the traumatic event. We'd made plenty of progress, but even with all that therapy, and with the passage of time, I was afraid I'd never truly forget what happened.

And despite how irrational it might have seemed, I still felt guilty about standing by while Uncle Steve drowned.

I dragged myself downstairs with the intention of coming up with an excuse to keep from going to my swimming lesson, but Mom seemed too on her game to be fooled. I downed a bowl of Cap'n Crunch and killed some time playing video games before I had to leave for the pool.

Mom dropped me off on her way to a job. I made her stop a block from the pool, just in case anyone happened by. I trudged the remaining distance in my slides with my towel draped over my shoulder, in no rush to get there. Probably unlike 99% of the other kids heading to the pool.

I waved at the lifeguard behind the counter, some guy I'd seen a million times but didn't know his name. Brandon something, maybe. The locker room was empty and quiet, save for the *drip-drip-drip* of a leaky showerhead and the hissing sound of a busted toilet. They'd both been broken for as long as I could remember. What was it about plumbing at public pools, anyway?

On the pool deck, I tossed my towel and slides onto a chair and looked around for Dante the Tormentor. I didn't see him, so I took a seat. He was probably out kicking puppies or squishing ladybugs to get in the mood to teach me. I closed my eyes and tried to get focused for the task ahead.

"Hello," a girl's voice said.

My eyes popped open. I shaded my face with my hands and squinted against the bright sunlight. A girl who looked an awful lot like Allie Merskie stood there, staring at me, a vague smile on her wonderful face.

"Uh, hey."

"You're Nick, right?"

"Yeah. Nick Carlin."

41

Her smile widened. "I'm Allie Merskie."

Yes, of course. What guy past puberty doesn't know you? "Hi."

"Are you ready?"

If Miller were here, something cheesy would have escaped his mouth, like "I was born ready." Luckily, he wasn't. "Uh, sure. I'm ready. I guess." I glanced around for Dante. "I have a, um, lesson with Dante this morning."

Her smile turned into a little frown—a cute one. "Didn't anyone tell you?"

"Tell me what?"

"Dante doesn't work here anymore. He got, well, he left."

"He left? What happened?"

Allie glanced around the pool deck and leaned closer, although we were alone. I got a whiff of her flowery-smelling shampoo. "He got caught smoking pot after the pool party Saturday night. They kicked him out."

Dante had been right; smoking would mess you up. It took a moment, but I finally put two and two together. "And you're..."

She stepped back and brightened. "Yep. I'm your new swim instructor."

Whoa!

We hopped into the pool, and I warmed up a bit, stretching my arms and legs, snapping my neck back and forth like a pro wrestler before getting into the ring. We were in about four feet of water, so I could stand easily.

"Okay, let's see where we're at. Show me what you've got," she said, pointing across the width of the pool to the other side. "Swim over there."

I took a deep breath and pushed off the wall. Head down in the water, I extended my right arm and pulled, then did the same with my left arm. Kicked for all I was worth. I tried to remember what Dante had told me about breathing. Blow out, then turn your head, and take a breath. Repeat.

I blew bubbles out through my nose, and when I ran out of air, I accidentally inhaled water up my nose. My legs stopped churning first, followed in short order by my arms. My feet hit bottom, and I stood, coughing and spitting. Shit! I turned around and looked back at my starting point. I'd only gone about fifteen feet. Allie hadn't moved, a sick smile on her face. She motioned me back.

I dog-paddled over. "Sorry."

"No need to apologize," she said. "But we've got some work to do. You need to learn to swim by when?"

We started by reviewing the fundamentals. For the bazillionth time in my life. But this time, the instructions were delivered with sensitivity and understanding. I mean, I was definitely swimming-challenged, and finally I had an instructor who realized that.

Plus she was Allie Merskie.

I paid close attention to each word she uttered and tried to duplicate every movement she demonstrated. It wasn't easy. I told her the nose-blowing technique wasn't working, so she suggested an alternative—exhale through my mouth. When she puckered up her lips to demonstrate, I just about keeled over. But I held it together, and after a few minutes, I was starting to understand things in a way I hadn't before. For the first time in a long time, I felt confident I really *could* learn how to swim. I pictured myself behind the wheels of a shiny red sports car, with Allie next to me in the passenger seat.

We kept at it, making progress, and toward the end of the lesson, she touched my shoulder. I felt like I'd been shocked with a thousand volts. "You're doing great. Why don't we try to put it all together now?"

"Sure." I held my arms above the water and shook them out. I adjusted my goggles and took a deep breath. Time for the proverbial sink or swim moment.

She gave me a thumbs up with one of her perfect thumbs. I nodded back and sucked in a huge breath. Holding it, I ducked and pushed off from the wall with my feet. Head down, I pulled with my right arm, then with my left. Feet churned the water behind me, a mini vortex. I propelled myself through the water.

Time to breathe. Slowly, I blew air bubbles out through my mouth, remembering to keep my arms and legs going. I was careful not to open my mouth too much. Just enough to squeeze the air out. So far, so good. I was doing it! I was swimming.

My breath was almost gone. Time to turn my head and fill up my lungs. My arms were in a rhythm now, my legs felt like an outboard motor. I turned my head and gulped. Instead of air, my mouth filled with water. I stopped swimming, stood up, and spit out a mouthful of disgusting chlorinated water. I slapped the surface of the pool with both open palms. Shit!

Allie swam over. "That was pretty good. Best swim of the day."

I threw my hands up. "Come on, I suck. Who are we kidding? I'm never going to learn how to swim."

She touched my shoulder. If she kept on touching me, I was going to have burn marks. "Don't be so hard on yourself. I've taught a lot of people how to swim. Some pick it up quicker than others. Doesn't mean anything."

I felt like a complete failure, on top of being a complete loser. I mean, how many sixteen-year-olds didn't know how to swim?

"Nick, you should relax. You'll learn. You just have to believe in yourself."

Uh-huh. I believed in myself. I believed I was never going to learn how to swim, no matter how many pep talks I got from Allie Merskie.

The picture of the red sports car in my mind dissolved, place taken by a rusted old bicycle. And Allie Merskie wasn't by my side.

Chapter Eight

That evening, Mom and I hunkered down at the kitchen table preparing a mass mailing. Every couple months, she mailed out a bunch of brochures advertising her pest control business. She figured most people probably pitched the brochure into the trash the minute they saw it, but enough potential customers gave her a call to make it worthwhile. As Mom always said, "Everybody has pests of one kind or another. They just don't know it."

On the ground next to my chair were two large boxes of pre-printed brochures. On one panel was a picture of a cockroach nibbling at a bit of food. Another panel showed a pair of mice next to a pantry door. And another featured a glossy picture of a menacing snake slithering toward a baby pool. That's the one Mom figured generated the most action. No one liked snakes, and no one liked putting their kids in danger. Never mind that most snakes around here were completely harmless. In fact, Mom said, snakes were good pest controllers themselves—they kept the mice away.

I pulled a stack of brochures from the box and passed half of them to Mom. I set the other half in front of me in a pile, squared up the edges, and peeled an address label off a sheet. I stuck *Anthony Adams* onto a brochure and smoothed my finger over the label, then placed the brochure in a plastic bin. Next to me, Mom did the same, although she was working from the other end of the alphabet.

"Nick-o, I'm sorry I haven't been around much lately. Work's been real busy, and you know me, I'm not one to turn down a job. Not as long as they pay me, of course." She used a fingernail to pry up the corner of a label and peeled it off.

"No sweat. I've been busy too."

"Oh yeah? Doing what?" She took her time positioning the label just so over the little address square printed on the brochure.

"Just, you know, hanging out and stuff."

"With Miller? How's he doing?"

"Miller is Miller. Need I say more?" I put another label in place. I didn't want to get into the threat his parents gave him about switching schools. She'd just ask me a million questions I didn't know the answers to.

"How was your lesson this morning?" She crumpled up an empty sheet of labels and tossed it into a trash bag we'd set on the floor between us.

"Okay," I said. "I got a new instructor."

Mom stopped what she was doing. "What? When I signed you up, I made sure I got the best one they had. What happened?"

"I guess Dante left." Mom already thought most of the kids my age—at least the ones she didn't know—were potheads. No sense adding fuel to her bonfire of suspicions; I'd never be able to go to another party again.

"How's the new one?"

"Huh?"

"How's the new instructor?"

"Okay." Peel, stick, smooth. Peel, stick, smooth. I concentrated on the task at hand.

"Good. What's his name?"

I kept my head down and kept peeling and sticking. "It's a her, Allie something."

"Oh, do I know her?" She casually picked up another sheet of labels and resumed working.

"I don't think so. She's a couple years older." I thought about telling Mom it was Allie who waved at us the other day in the Bugmobile, but I knew Mom and her questions.

"Well, as long as she's good. You know how important this is, both the swimming and the driving. Achieving goals builds character. Plus, if I'm paying for these lessons, I want the best teacher they've got. You know what I mean?"

"Yeah sure, Mom."

"You need to stick up for yourself in this world. Get what you want. If you don't, people will take advantage of you." She pointed to me. "That's how things work, Nick-o. Don't forget that."

We worked in silence for a few minutes. My pile of labeled brochures grew at a steady rate, while the size of Mom's hardly changed. I grabbed another stack of brochures from the box and put them on the table in front of me. Mom still had plenty.

"How did Gram seem to you yesterday?"

"Like she always does."

"That bad?" Mock horror crept onto Mom's face, then she broke into a grin. "What is wrong with that lady, anyhow?"

"She was fine." I picked up another sheet of labels, while Mom looked on. What, was I the only one working here?

"Well, she's seemed a little...off lately. I hope she's feeling okay. I think something's up with her."

"Like what?"

"I don't know. She keeps secrets from me. By the way, she called today asking for you. Said something about moving furniture for her this week." Mom picked at one of her fingernails.

"Again? I moved stuff around last week. And some of her stuff is really heavy."

"She also said there's a problem with her computer."

I was the family's IT expert. Although I had to give it to Gram, she knew more about computers than Mom did. "Okay. I'll take a look. In a few days." A little bit of Gram went a long way, and I'd just gotten my fill.

"Thanks, dear. Remember, while you're there, scout around a little. See if you can find out what she's up to."

Is this how Jason Bourne got started? His mother made him spy on his grandmother? "Sure, whatever."

"How are we doing on the brochures?"

I checked the box, and there were plenty left. "Another hour and a half, at least." After sticking on the labels, we still had to stamp them all.

"Uh-huh. Well, let's keep at it."

We worked in silence some more. In the past, we often listened to the radio or hooked my phone up to some speakers, but we usually ended up arguing about what songs to listen to. No one argued with silence.

"So, gone on any good dates lately?"

Of course, the trouble with silence was Mom felt compelled to fill it with questions. "Not really."

"What does 'not really' really mean? That you've been on a date that wasn't good, or that you've had some good times, but they weren't really dates?" Again, Mom put down the labels she was working on and leaned back in her chair.

"Nothing. 'Not really' means nothing."

"Okay, okay. Didn't mean to pry."

I grunted something back at her. Mom couldn't help prying any more than a hummingbird couldn't help humming. She must have gotten the pry gene from Gram.

"I need a little break." She got up and went to the fridge. "Want something to drink? Soda?"

"No. I'm good."

Mom returned with a Diet Coke and popped it open. Took a long slug. The liquid gurgled as it went down her throat. I kept peeling and sticking.

Between sips, Mom asked, "I know it's only been a few days, but how are things going with you and Jason?"

I bit the inside of my lip as I peeled off another label. "Fine, I guess."

"I didn't hear much about Beltway Saturday. It go okay?"

"Yeah, fine."

"That's good. It's important to me that the two men in my life get along, you know."

Peel, stick, smooth. "Uh huh." Truth be told, Jason hadn't been around much. I think he still had stuff to take care of at his apartment before he officially, completely, moved in here. I wasn't sure; I tried not to talk to him. "Where is he now?"

Mom drained some more of her soda. "He said he was going out with some buddies."

"He *said*? You make it sound like you don't believe him."

"What? No, of course I believe him." Mom chewed on her lip and stared off into space like she did when I said something she needed to digest. Then her face brightened. "I've got some good news."

I could use some good news for a change. "What?"

"We're going on vacation." She winked at me.

"When?"

"This weekend. I got Mack Attack to fill in. We'll leave Friday afternoon, come back Sunday."

Mack Mason was a college kid who liked to kill bugs. Actually, he liked using the sprayer. Mom employed him during busy times or when we went away. "Great. Ocean City or Virginia Beach?" Every year, we'd head to the beach for a few days. The ocean. The boardwalk.

The bikinis. "Hey, can I bring someone?"

Mom's smile faded. "I thought we'd try someplace else this year.

A sour feeling grew in my gut. "Where?"

"West Virginia. There's a place Jason likes. Hiking in the woods, stuff like that. Should be a nice change."

Jason? When I was younger, vacations usually meant Mom and me. Sometimes I'd bring a friend, and sometimes she'd bring a friend, but she'd never brought along a serious boyfriend. This was going to royally suck.

"Nick? How does that sound?"

I snapped back to the present. "Huh? Oh, I guess it sounds okay." The words came out pretty flat as visions of boring hikes replaced those of sunbathing on the beach.

Mom pushed back her chair and walked behind mine. She draped her arms around my neck. Her hair tickled my ear. "Listen, Nick-o. Having Jason around will take some getting used to. Things will be different. Not worse, but different. I thought all of us taking a vacation together would give you an opportunity to get to know him better. Can you keep an open mind and give him a chance? I know you'll like him. I mean, I'm your mom and I like him, right?" She kissed the top of my head.

I swallowed. "Yeah, okay. I'm sure we'll get along great." I hoped she couldn't smell the uncertainty—and resentment—oozing from my pores. For so long—twelve years now—it had just been me and my mom.

When I was almost four years old—two years before Uncle Steve's death—my father died. Unlike my uncle, though, he didn't die from natural causes. He was killed in a car accident. Some asshole driver, high as a kite, ran a stop sign and T-boned him. Some kid who'd just gotten his license decided to get stoned and go out joyriding. Going too fast, lost control, plowed right into my dad's car. Both of them died.

I knew his accident was one of the reasons Mom was so overprotective when she took me out driving. Why she micromanaged my lessons. Why she wanted me to stay in the right lanes and never exceed the speed limit. I didn't exactly blame her, but...

I didn't remember much about my dad, not from my actual memories, although I seemed to know about a lot of stuff he did, from all the stories Mom used to tell about him.

That was one of the things I held against Jason. Ever since he'd come onto the scene, Mom didn't talk about my father so much. Even this many years after his death, I missed that.

And now I had to go on vacation with Jason, as if we were some kind of family.

"Thanks, hon." She kissed my head again, then broke off her hug. "I'm beat. I'm going up to bed. Do me a favor, will you? Go down and feed the gang?"

"Sure, Mom. Goodnight."

* * *

When people first meet my mother and find out what she does for a living, they're surprised. Pest control isn't what you'd typically think of as "a woman's job." After the initial shock wears off, people lock in on a stereotype. She must be a tough cookie to go after insects and spiders and rats and snakes. She must be heartless to kill little defenseless animals. She must be a little off-kilter to want to be an *exterminator*.

Of course, if anyone says the "e" word to my mother's face, they'll get a mouthful. She's a pest control expert, not an *exterminator*. People never make that mistake twice.

What they don't know about my mother is how soft-hearted she can be. When she wants to be, that is. She's kind of a Dr. Jekyll and Mrs.

Hyde of the pest control business—her sympathetic feeling comes and goes. When it goes, she has no trouble killing pests. But when her soft-heart takes over...

I flipped the light switch on and descended the basement steps. At the bottom, a thousand eyes—most of which were compound—turned in my direction. About three dozen aquariums, boxes, jars, and other makeshift cages shared the unfurnished room with the furnace and water heater. The enclosures were full of rescued pests.

Hundreds of crickets chirped in an old fish tank topped with netting. Scores of spiders spun their webs in another used aquarium. Smaller jars held thousands of assorted insects: three or four different types of ants, roaches, centipedes, assorted beetle-looking-things, and a bunch of other creepy crawlers I couldn't identify. I'm not sure Mom could either. Not that she cared; everything was welcome with the exception of termites. Those, she always hated.

Across the room, twenty mice huddled together in a glass cage, a breathing gray-brown ball of fluff. Next to the mice, two black snakes slept in side-by-side coils. A full-sized rectangle of poster board hung between the two cages. Mom thought the barrier, along with five Christmas tree air fresheners thumbtacked to the poster board, would keep the snakes from realizing their dinner—and breakfast and lunch— was a mere two feet away. Who knew if it worked? The snakes usually looked pretty sleepy to me.

The population—types and numbers—of the menagerie varied. Sometimes Mom would bring something new home from work, and we'd have to let something go to make room. More times than not, however, especially lately, whenever she adopted a new batch of immigrants, I'd have to go out to the garage or up to the attic and find another cage.

I dumped some old vegetable peelings into the cricket house and threw some stale Honey Nut Cheerios in with the ants. I unscrewed the top to a small jar full of black ants and, using a popsicle stick, flicked some into the spider cage. I kept hoping Mom would find a tarantula someday and bring it home, but she said it's unlikely she'll find one around here—unless someone keeping one as a pet lets it go or something.

After feeding the insects, I made sure all the cage lids were secure, then walked over to the other side of the room.

The mice also got a couple handfuls of Cheerios, but I didn't have to feed the snakes tonight—they got their meal a few days ago, and a mouse will last a while. I observed the snakes for a moment. Black, lethargic, mysterious. Good for what exactly, except creeping people out? Watching them with their dull, flat, reptilian eyes, and forked tongues, I couldn't help but think of Jason.

Chapter Nine: T-minus 11 days

Better Get Cracking

I slogged over to the lounge chair, tired and wet. I'd just spent thirty minutes practicing. Breathing. Kicking. The stroke. All separately, all in combination. At times, it felt like I was getting the hang of it. Other times, I remained a proud representative of anchors everywhere.

When I tried swimming the width of the pool, I made it about two-thirds of the way. A new record. So at least I had that going for me.

Picking up my towel, I glanced at the clock—one-thirty. Miller should be arriving any minute. Ever since Monday's lesson with Allie, I'd been trying to contact him, to tell him the news. But he'd been grounded. Something about posting too-candid pictures of his sisters on Twitter.

I sat in the chair and dried my hair. When it wasn't dripping any more, I handcombed it to remove the tangles. Then I donned a pair of shades and reclined, content to watch the sun worshippers for a while.

In addition to Miller's grounding, he lost his computer and cell phone privileges. Again. When I'd called the landline, his mother said he wasn't available and he "wouldn't be receiving visitors." Whatever. His suspension had lifted this morning, and rather than tell him over the phone, I asked him to meet me here. It would be nice to see his face when he heard Allie Merskie would be giving me some personal attention instead of dickhead Dante.

Almost on cue, Miller ambled out onto the pool deck. Dressed in a pair of bright yellow board shorts and a black t-shirt, he reminded me of a bumblebee. Over one shoulder, he had a purple beach towel, while a mesh tote bag—with fake yellow plastic flowers—hung over the other one. A floppy old-lady hat sat atop his curly hair. All in all, he looked ridiculous. I noticed all the other pool-goers making faces as Miller came my way. How could someone so concerned about getting laid dress like that?

"Hey, there, Saint Nick." He dropped his mesh bag on the ground and began spreading his beach towel on the chaise lounge next to mine. "What's going on?"

"Sit down, I've got something to tell you."

Miller frowned at me and plopped down on his chair. He pushed the edge of his hat out of his eyes. "Okay. I'm all ears, mon ami."

I glanced around, making sure no one could hear, and leaned toward Miller. "I know you're not going to believe this, but Allie Merskie is my new swimming instructor."

Miller's eyes turned into dinner plates. "Holy shit." Then he smiled. "Bullshit. You're putting me on. Asshole." But the amazement didn't completely drain from his face.

I just stared at him.

"You're not bullshitting me. Holy shit. What happened to Muscle-Man Tanner?"

"He got fired. For smoking pot or something."

Miller licked his lips. "Man. Allie Merskie. I think I'm going to have to start coming to your swimming lessons."

I leaned back and crossed my arms across my chest. "Fat chance."

"This puts a lot of pressure on you, you know. If you don't learn how to swim, you're going to look like the biggest wuss around. In front of her." One side of his mouth went up.

I hadn't thought about it like that. I thought I looked like a wuss anyway—a sixteen-year-old who couldn't swim. But a sixteen-year-old who couldn't *learn* how to swim, a failure, was even worse. "Man, you're right. Crap. What am I going to do? Me and water…" Snatches of my dream the other night mixed with actual memories of the accident. Goosebumps crawled up one arm and down the other. My heart raced.

"Dude, get a grip. You're trembling."

I opened my eyes—I didn't even know I'd closed them—and focused on Miller's chubby face. Slowly, I felt normal again. "Uh, yeah. I'm okay. I'm not gonna fail. I'll learn how to swim if it kills me."

"You don't learn how to swim and you don't get your license, you'll wish you were dead," Miller said.

A shadow fell over us from behind. I turned around and Pool Czar Ternikiwicz stood there, stooped over, a squint on her wrinkled face and balled fists on her hips. "No horseplay with you two." Her Eastern European accent was so thick I could barely understand what she said.

"No horseplay. Got it."

Miller nodded, too startled to say anything.

The Pool Czar squinted even harder, until her eyes disappeared. "People come here to relax, so to remember, no roughhousing." She pointed a bony finger at us. "I have my eyes on you. Remember this always."

"Yes, ma'am. We'll behave. Promise."

After a curt nod, she turned on her heels and stalked off.

"Who was that?" Miller asked.

"The Pool Czar. Everyone calls her P.Z. behind her back." Evidently, some genius couldn't spell czar.

"You could have warned me."

"If you came to the pool more often, you'd know who she was. You can relax, though; she's old and harmless. Unless you mess with her. She schedules swim lessons and runs the swim team. Scares the crap out of the little kids. She thinks she runs the rest of the pool, too." The pool's swim team wins the regionals every year, so the pool manager puts up with her terrorizing the members.

"Where's she from anyway? Russia?"

I shrugged. "Could be. I think she swam in the Olympics for some Eastern European country. Way back."

"And what's with the hunchback deal? Her first name Eileen?"

"Funny." P.Z. did stand a little crooked. "She's old. Ancient. Cut her some slack."

"How can the kids even understand her? Sheesh." Something caught Miller's attention, and his head swiveled. He pointed at the locker room entrance. "Hey, it's Laura. Is she stalking you, or what?" He took off his hat and waved it like a signal flag.

Laura waved back and headed our way. I adjusted my shades.

"Hey, guys," she said. "Nice day for a swim."

"I guess." To me, no day was nice for swimming. But I didn't want to sound like a downer.

"Hey, where's your cousin?" Miller asked.

"She left. Went back home." She turned her head and winked at me. "Too bad, she really was into you. In fact, after we saw you at the mall, she kept saying she hoped you'd call her. I guess you were too busy. Oh, well, she'll be back in a couple years."

Miller stared at Laura, unsure if she were serious. I wish I'd thought of it—few things were more enjoyable than yanking Miller's chain.

"Your loss, Miller." Laura bent down and patted Miller on his beefy calf. Then she straightened and spoke to me. "Doing some practicing today?"

"I was. Taking a breather."

"Sure. You don't want to get too tired. Throws off your stroke, right?"

"Yeah. I guess." In the background, the lifeguard blew his whistle, indicating adult swim was over and it was okay for the kids to recapture the pool.

"Are you here alone?" Miller seemed to have recovered from the shock of his lost lust.

"I'm supposed to meet Bethany and Rhee here." She glanced around. "Have you seen them?"

"Nope," I said.

"And believe me, we would have noticed," Miller added. "Girls like that..."

"Shut up, Miller," Laura and I said at practically the same time.

Miller made a face. "They're not here, so you can hang with us," he said to Laura. "If you don't mind slumming, that is."

"Well..." Laura turned her head toward me and raised an eyebrow in Miller's direction. "I'd better not. Bethany and Rhee..."

"Sure. No sweat," I said, wondering not for the first time how many social opportunities Miller cost me over the years.

"You *all* could join us," Miller said.

Laura's mouth puckered. "Hmm. I don't think so. Maybe next time."

"Okay. Your loss," Miller muttered, just loud enough for Laura to hear.

With a parting roll of her eyes, Laura walked to the other side of the pool and started arranging a few lounge chairs and setting her stuff out.

"She totally wants you." Miller pushed his sunglasses up on his nose. "I tried to get her to stay, but..."

Across the pool, Laura peeled her t-shirt off. She wore a black bikini top that accentuated a pretty good tan. Miller clicked his tongue as she wiggled out of her white shorts to expose her bikini bottom. "Nice.

Very nice," Miller whispered. "You should be tapping that, dude."

"Shut up, Miller. Stop acting like a dick or you'll never get what you want."

He flipped me off. More evidence to support my case. Sometimes I wondered why I even hung around with him, but we'd been friends since second grade, and he'd come to my defense more times than I could count—on the playground, in the school hallways, during lunch periods—as we battled the inevitable bullies. I guessed I'd always have his back, if push came to shove.

Thirty feet away, to our left, the creaky half-height door to the pool office opened and Allie Merskie emerged. She sported her usual lifeguard suit, the teal one-piece, and she twirled a whistle lanyard around her finger. First one way, then the other. Next to me, Miller sucked in some air.

Miller said a few words, but the only thing in the forefront of my brain was Allie. She walked toward us, twirling her whistle. When she came to our chairs, she stopped and opened her perfect mouth. "Hi Nick." She smiled at Miller. "Hi Miller."

Miller took off his ridiculous hat and put it on his stomach. "Hey."

"Is Kelly around these days?"

"Yeah. Well, sort of. She's around, but she's always with Nathaniel. Like a hairy Siamese twin or something." He blinked a few times.

Allie nodded. "Tell her I said hi, 'k?"

"Sure." Miller's tongue was practically on his chest.

Allie turned to me. "I'm glad to see you here, Nick. I hope you're working on what we went over yesterday."

"Uh, yeah. That's exactly what I'm doing. Was doing. I'm just taking a little break before I get right back to it. You know, practicing." My tongue seemed to get stuck in my mouth.

"Good, good. If you have any questions, come find me. I'll be in the chair for a while now, but then I'll be in the office."

"Sure." My cheeks were getting warm, and it wasn't from the sun. "Thanks."

Allie turned to head off toward the lifeguard chair. Before she took a step, she turned back. "Oh, I almost forgot. I heard you were good at math."

"You did?" Now my entire face was aflame. Why had she been talking about me?

"Well, are you?"

"Uh, I guess." In grade school, people used to call me the computer because I could add and subtract faster than you could punch the numbers into a calculator.

"Well, my little brother Colin, step-brother actually, needs some help in math. And he won't listen to anyone in the family. So my mom thought we should try getting him a tutor."

"I don't know..." Helping Allie's brother sounded great, but...

"It's not like he's behind in math. He's trying to get ahead. He's really smart, but he needs a little help focusing. And he never listens to us. My mom thought it would be good if someone outside the family worked with him." She tossed the whistle up in the air a few inches and caught it. "So? What do you think?"

Out of the corner of my eye, I saw Miller nodding his head. Small nods, but rapid. "Uh. Sure."

"Great." Allie beamed. "Can you come over tomorrow, say 3:00? Colin will be back from soccer camp by then."

"Sounds good."

"I can give you directions after tomorrow's lesson." She said goodbye to us and headed for the lifeguard chair to relieve the guard on duty.

"Dude, whatever you're drinking, I want some," Miller said.

I stretched out on the chaise and put my hands behind my head. On the other side of the pool deck, I noticed Laura spreading sunscreen on herself. After a minute, she got up and asked the lady in the next chair over to do her back.

Damn Miller!

Chapter Ten: T-minus 10 days

Concentrate

I followed the directions Allie had given me after my lesson, and I skidded my bike to a stop on her driveway at three minutes to three. I marched up to the front door, hoping to get a glimpse of her. She'd said she would probably be there to introduce me to her brother before she went shopping. I poked the doorbell with my index finger.

A few moments later, the door swung open to reveal Allie. She wore tight white shorts and a pink t-shirt with little frills on the sleeves. This was the first time I'd seen her when she wasn't wearing a swimsuit, and I wasn't disappointed. She seemed a lot older in street clothes.

"Hi there." She stepped back. "Come on in."

"Sure." Their house was bigger than ours—much bigger—and I found myself standing in an ornately decorated two-story foyer. A black grand piano gleamed at me from an adjoining room.

"Just a sec." She craned her head toward the curved staircase. "Colin. Your tutor's here," she bellowed. "He'll be down in a minute. Come on, I'll show you where you'll be."

She jerked her head, and I followed her down the hall, through the kitchen, through the dining room, through a living room, and through some other room with two blue leather sofas. Finally, we entered a small room containing an old, wooden table with two chairs. "This is it. Our little study room."

A few posters adorned the walls, and bookshelves lined two sides of the room. A clock, just like the ones that hung in classrooms everywhere, was positioned over the doorway. "This is where we go when we want some peace and quiet. It's far removed from all the commotion in the house."

I nodded. No TV, no computer. This place *was* isolated.

Allie pointed to a math textbook on the table. Next to it was a pad of paper and a few pencils. "You like Algebra?"

"I guess. Better than Geometry. I hated doing proofs."

She smiled. "I'm with you there."

We heard him before we saw him, thunderous footsteps fast approaching. A short, skinny boy burst through the doorway, his size at odds with the stomping. The only thing big on him was his scowl.

"Nick, this is Colin," Allie said. "Colin, this is Nick." The wider she smiled, the more Colin scowled.

"Hey Colin."

Colin gave me a half-nod, and the scowl morphed into a sneer.

Allie raised an eyebrow and spoke to me in a calm, measured tone. "Nick, Colin is going into eighth grade. He's taking Algebra online so he'll be ready for Geometry in the fall. Can you go through his last two assignments with him and start working on the next one?" She sounded like a tour guide at the zoo, trying not to spook the wild animals while she talked about them.

I smiled at Colin and mimicked Allie's even voice. "Colin, it's nice to meet you. I'll be happy to go over your assignments with you and help you in any way I can. Sound good?"

Colin rolled his eyes. "How 'bout we cut the crap and get started?" He glanced at the clock. "We got exactly one hour, right? I mean, that's all I agreed to."

Allie's smile faltered, just a hair. "That's right, one hour." She swallowed and glanced uneasily in my direction. "So...I guess I'll leave you two to your math. The mall awaits." She mouthed the words, "Good luck," to me before she left.

A bad feeling grew in my gut. "Okay, then. Why don't we get started?" I picked up the textbook and flipped to the table of contents. "Which chapter are you on?"

Colin put his feet up on the table and tipped the chair back until only two legs were on the floor. "Thanks, but I've got everything under control."

"Okay. Why don't you show me what you know? We can start right at the beginning." I flipped to the review problems at the end of the first chapter. "How about number one?"

A grin slowly grew on Colin's face. "Look, I've already done all the problems. I know Algebra." He made no move to look at the problem in the textbook.

"Well, if you know Algebra, how hard would it be to show me by doing a few problems?"

Colin glanced at the clock on the wall. "Fifty-seven minutes. Tick-tock, tick-tock."

"Colin, we might as well do some math. Your parents are paying me to help you." Even at thirty bucks an hour, this might not be worth it.

"How about this? You leave now, and I won't tell. Then we'll both be happy. Tick-tock." He shifted, and I could read the words written on his t-shirt. *Just Don't Do It.*

"*I* won't be happy. Come on, let's just do a few problems. You want to get a good grade, right?"

"I don't need your help to get a good grade. I told you, I know this stuff." He crossed his arms across his chest.

"Then why do your parents think you need a tutor?"

Colin snorted. "My dad couldn't care less about my grades. It's my step-mom who wants this. And she's only on my case because I'm not her kid. I embarrass her."

"I'm sure that's not true."

"How the heck would you know? And trust me, it's true. I'm a pimple on her botoxed butt." Another glance at the clock. "Fifty-four minutes. Tick-tock."

This was starting to veer pretty far from Algebra. I made a big show of sighing. "Tell you what, let's do some math, then we'll stop early, and I won't tell your mom, okay?"

"Step-mom." He glared at me. "I'll tell *you* what. We can sit here staring at each other if you want, but I'm not doing any Algebra." He strung out the word *Al-gee-bra*.

I sighed again, this time for real. My first tutoring assignment, and I couldn't even get my pupil to do a single problem. Maybe I should just get up and leave. But what would Allie think? That I'm a failure in the pool *and* as a tutor? That I couldn't handle her little brother? "What's it going to take to get you to do some math here?"

Colin narrowed his eyes. "I know why you're doing this."

"What?"

"Tutoring me."

"To help you with your Algebra. So you can take Geometry this year."

He grinned. "No. Why you're *really* doing it. Because you have the hots for Allie."

My breath caught. "What? That's not why." The words came out thin.

"Hey, why should you be different?" He ticked the names off on his fingers. "Last year, it was Julio and Spencer. Then Jerome, and B.K., and Tommy. Plus, there's always that big goon, Blake. I could go on."

I held up my hand. "It's not like that at all. She's just my swimming instructor."

"Yeah, right. You're like every other guy out there. After my step-sister. I don't blame you." He winked at me. "You're not denying that, are you?"

"I'm here to help you with your math. And make thirty bucks. That's all."

"Then how come your face is so red? You are so busted!"

This time, I was the one who glanced at the clock. Forty-two minutes left. This had become more painful than swimming lessons. Was I going to let this thirteen-year-old get the best of me? *No freaking way.* I slid a pad of paper in front of me and started scribbling. "If you're not going to do any work, I might as well start filling out your evaluation form."

"The what?" Colin took his feet off the desk and the chair clunked to the ground. "Evaluation form?"

"You bet. Your step-mom requires it. Ordinarily, I don't believe in ratting out my students, but…well, she insisted on getting a complete report. I seem to recall her saying something about 'getting grounded.'" I stopped writing for a moment and tapped the pencil on my chin. Then I put it to the paper and muttered as I wrote, "Complete disrespect for me and—"

"Hey, hey. Just a second." The scowl had disappeared, and an expression bordering on panic had taken its place. "I was just messing with you. Having a little fun, you know?"

I kept scribbling. "Hmm. I'm not sure about that. Let's see, 'Refused to cooperate.'"

"Nick, wait. Seriously. I'm ready now." He picked up a pencil and grabbed at the textbook. He fumbled with the pages, trying to get to the end of the first chapter. "What number should I start with?"

I tilted my head and stared at him. "Are there going to be any more, uh, difficulties?"

Colin shook his head. "No. I promise. Sorry." He swallowed and kept his gaze on the paper in front of me. "Can you wait until the end to write the evaluation? Please? Give me another chance?"

I waited a second, then pushed the fake evaluation form to the other side of the table. "Let's just leave it there for now. If you're ready, why don't we start with problem number one?"

The remaining forty-seven minutes went without a hitch. *Tick-tock.*

* * *

On my way home from tutoring, I swung by Gram's to take care of her chores. I'd told her I'd be coming by tomorrow, but I figured she'd be around. She didn't get out much.

When I rode up, a strange car was parked behind her fifteen-year-old Taurus in the driveway. Another Taurus, although it looked a bit newer.

I rapped on the door and waited. Put my ear to the door. Nothing.

I knocked again, louder. Sometimes, Gram had the TV on at ultra-high volume. Maybe she and her friend were watching Oprah or something.

After another minute, I rang the bell. Inside, I heard it chime, but I didn't hear anyone call out.

I went around to the side of the house and leaned over the fence. Not there, so I went back to the front door and rang the bell again. Where could she be? A vision of her, lying facedown on the kitchen floor, sent my pulse pumping. I banged on the door. She was always there when I came by.

"Hold your horses," I heard her call from inside. That was followed by the sound of the deadbolt being unlocked. The door cracked open, and a portion of Gram's face appeared. As soon as she saw it was me, she brightened and opened the door so I could see her whole face. "Nicky. How are you? Is it Thursday already?"

"No. Still Wednesday. I was in the neighborhood and thought I'd drop by."

"Well, you should have called first."

"Sorry. I came to move that stuff and fix your computer."

"Sure, sure. I'm just..." Her voice diminished.

"Whose car is that?" I asked.

"Car? What car?"

I pointed at the Taurus behind hers. "That car. The brown one."

"Oh. *That* car." She chewed on her lip, just like Mom did. "A friend's."

"You okay, Gram?" Maybe Mom was right, maybe Gram was beginning to lose it. We needed that like we needed a case of Ebola.

Gram blew her breath out. "You're sixteen, right?"

"Yeah."

"Okay, then." The door opened all the way, and Gram stood there in a bright red robe cinched at the waist with a silky-looking sash.

"Did I wake you?"

"No, dear. Come on in."

I followed her into the sunroom, where we'd chatted the other day. But someone was sitting in the spot where I'd sat. A scrawny old dude in a pair of black boxers and a sleeveless t-shirt. "Howdy," he said, getting up.

"Uh, hi." I looked at Gram, but she just shrugged. He extended his hand, and I shook it, gently, not wanting to damage anything.

"Herb Conroy."

"I'm Nick. Her grandson."

"Well, howdy again," Herb said. He wasn't wearing any socks, and his toenails were a little on the yellow side. "It's a pleasure. I guess I don't have to tell you what a great grandma you have." Herb exchanged a look with Gram, and I just about lost my lunch. Was everyone in my family getting laid except me? *But Gram?*

"Oh yeah, she's something else." Today had turned into quite the awkward day. "I think maybe I should be going. Nice meeting—" I started to leave, wondering how I was going to get the image of Herb out of my head.

"Hold on there, Nicky," Gram said. "You're already here. And Herb can give you a hand moving the furniture. What do you think, hon?"

Herb and I said, "Okay" at the exact same time. My skin crawled just thinking about it.

"Good. Now come along."

"Hang on a second," Herb said. "I'd better put my shoes on." He left the room.

When Herb was gone, Gram whispered. "So, what do you think of him?"

Oh, where to begin? "He seems nice enough. But, Gram, I don't—"

"He's a doll." She batted her eyelashes, and it looked like she'd gotten a piece of dirt in her eyes.

"Listen, Gram, it's really none of my—"

"Shush. Here he comes." Gram jabbed a finger to her lips and smoothed her robe with the other hand.

Herb returned wearing a pair of brown wingtips. Sleeveless t-shirt, black boxers, brown wingtips without socks. He could give Miller a run for his money in a worst-dressed competition.

"Follow me, gents." Gram led us upstairs. I closed my eyes when we passed the open door to her bedroom. She took us down the hall to the guest bedroom. "I want that dresser to go against that wall. And let's try the desk there." She directed us with hand gestures.

I took my place at one side of the dresser, while Herb started toward the far side. He stumbled halfway there but caught himself before he toppled over. "You okay?" asked Gram.

"Sure, sure." He dusted himself off, like they did in the movies, although he hadn't gotten anywhere close to actually hitting the floor.

"You know, I think I might be able to move this myself," I said. In fact, I was pretty sure I *had* moved this exact dresser a few months ago, all by myself.

"Nonsense," Herb said, taking up a position on the other side. "The two of us will make quick work of this." He curled his fingers under one of the drawer supports. "When I say three, we'll lift it and carry it over. Got it?"

"Sure." I got a good hold of the dresser and flexed my knees. "Ready when you are."

"Okay. One. Two." Herb let go of the dresser and stood, flexing his hands. "Sorry. Cramped up." He glanced at Gram. Smiled. Then he grabbed onto the dresser again. "Okie dokie. One. Two. Three!"

On three, we both lifted the dresser. Except his side didn't lift. I could see the muscles—such that they were—all the way up his arms tense and heard a little grunt, but his side of the dresser never got airborne. After about fifteen seconds, I set my side down. "Hang on. I need a sec." I flexed my own hands and shook them out a bit. "I see what you mean. Hard on the hands. This thing is heavy."

Herb backed away from the dresser and mopped some imaginary sweat from his brow with the back of a hand. "Whew. Barb, doll, you sure there aren't some gold bricks hidden in the dresser somewhere?" Herb's face had taken on a pinkish-purple hue.

"Just a minute, boys," Gram said, putting a hand to her chin. "I'm seeing things in a different light now." She walked around the dresser, tilting her head this way and that, clucking to herself. "I'll be right back. Don't move a thing!" Gram darted out of the room, as much as someone that old can dart.

Herb smiled at me, still massaging his hands. "Your grandma's a terrific gal. So warm and considerate. I knew I'd like her the moment I read her profile."

"Her profile?" I was starting to get that uneasy feeling again, the one in the pit of my stomach when I was about to hear things I didn't want to hear.

He nodded. "At MatureMatesForLife.com."

"Where?"

Herb looked shocked. "Online. That's where we met. You didn't know?"

"No, I didn't know Gram was..." I wondered if there was some kind of pill you could take that would wipe out your memory of the past hour.

"Oh. I just assumed that...well, Barb said you help with her computer and stuff. I thought you knew." He gave an uneasy laugh.

"Nope. News to me."

"Oh. Well. No big deal, right? Isn't that how kids meet these days?" *Not this kid.* "Sure. Some do, I guess."

"Anyway, it's been the best three weeks I've had in a long time, getting to know your grandma."

Three weeks and this guy's already walking around Gram's house in boxers and wingtips sans socks? A vision of myself in fifty years flashed through my mind. Would I be like Herb?

"She's got a lot of energy, that one. Quite the spitfire."

"Uh, I guess." The vise in my stomach continued tightening.

"Why just the other day..." He clammed up, and his face seemed even more flushed. "Yes indeed, she's something else."

Luckily, Gram popped back into the room carrying a large doily and two red candles in fancy brass candleholders. She spread the doily on top of the dresser and placed the candlesticks atop the doily. Then she shifted them back and forth a few times—each adjustment was only a fraction of a millimeter—until they were aligned. "Perfect. That's just what this room needed. And now, the dresser looks fine right where it is."

Herb exhaled loudly. "Well, then. I guess our work is done." He winked at me and stuck out his hand again. "Nice job, partner."

71

I shook it, trying to ignore the slight tremor in his hand, hoping it was simply a remnant of the recent exertion. "Yeah, partner," I said, again careful not to squeeze too hard. "Nice job."

Chapter Eleven

A few hours later, I was home getting creamed in Call of Duty when I got mercifully interrupted by a text message from Laura. She was bored and wanted to hang out at the pond. I told her I was bored, too—although I would have hung out with her regardless—and we agreed to meet there in fifteen minutes. I left a note for Mom on the kitchen counter and hopped on my bike for the short ride.

In the center of the next subdivision over was a pretty cool spot, the Charles G. Pettigrew Park. I didn't know who Mr. Pettigrew was, but he put his name on a nice place to spend some time. On one side of the park stood a playground, some tennis courts, and a basketball full-court. On the other side were baseball and soccer fields. An undeveloped stretch of land—mostly trees—connected the two sides. Asphalt trails wound through the woods and circled two large duck ponds.

When I was a toddler, Mom would bring me to the playground, and I'd climb around on the plastic equipment until I'd skin my knee and start bawling. As I got older, she'd still bring me, but I got better with my climbing and graduated to the more advanced playground stuff like the zipline and monkey bars. Eventually, Mom stopped bringing me, but I'd walk or ride my bike over to play soccer or shoot hoops.

It wasn't until I reached middle school that I started coming here just to hang around with my friends after school. We found an isolated spot on a little fishing dock built at the far end of the farthest pond where no one bothered us. The cast of characters was ever-changing, although it was usually me, Miller, Johnny B, and Hairy Larry, before he moved to Miami at the end of seventh grade.

Things got a lot more exciting, of course, when girls started hanging around with us. In the years before seventh grade, we'd always tried to avoid being around girls whenever we could. But, as Miller used to say, we grew some hair on our balls.

Kayla Wilson, Emily Sun, Tatiani Ivan-something, and the girl with the henna tattoos whose name I'm not sure I ever knew would show up from time to time. Of course, Laura was a regular, too. It was almost always at least two or three of them. I couldn't remember many times when just a single girl would come. I guess hanging out with us was kind of like going to the bathroom—strength in numbers. Or maybe they were just afraid someday Miller would be the only guy to show up.

Anyway, it had been a while since I'd been to the pond. As I biked over there, I wondered why Laura picked that spot.

I passed the playground first, and things looked like they always did. Parents and nannies sitting on the benches watching their tots negotiate the slides and fireman's poles. A few kids were playing b-ball, and a quartet of middle-aged ladies was arguing about something on one of the tennis courts.

After I passed the tennis courts, the path forked, and I headed toward the far pond. In a clearing to my right, a bunch of kids—older than elementary age but not yet in high school—were sitting on the grass, laughing and poking at each other. The higher-pitched laughter of the girls reminded me of when I was one of those kids just a few years ago.

I rounded the last bend in the path, and the small, wooden dock came into view. I left the path and bounced along the grass, careful to maneuver my bike around some serious clumps of gooseshit. They called these duck ponds, but the only birds I ever saw were geese—and lots of them.

Laura stood on her tiptoes at the end of the dock, leaning over the rail, her back toward me. She was probably looking at one of the creatures inhabiting the pond. Aside from the ever-present geese, there were all sorts of animals—fish, frogs, snakes, turtles, foxes, groundhogs, and more—in the pond and surrounding woods. It was quite the suburban nature preserve. As I got closer, she heard my bike crunching twigs and spun around. When she saw it was me and not some maniac stalker, she waved and flashed a big smile. Her clothing defined summer—navy shorts, a white top, and flip-flops. "Hi," she called out.

I braked to a stop and ditched my bike on the ground. Trotted over. "Hey there." I hugged her, then broke it off. "How's it going?"

"Good." She pointedly looked over my shoulder. "Where's your sidekick?"

"Who, Miller?"

"Yeah, who else?"

"I don't know." Had she wanted me to bring him along? I pulled out my phone. "Should I see what he's doing?"

Her hand touched mine, and an electric shock ran halfway up my arm, equal in force to the one I got when Allie had touched me. "No. That's okay. Just wondering. I'm not really in a 'Miller' mood today."

"I understand. Sometimes I feel the same way." Lately, I was feeling that way more and more, but I didn't confess that to Laura. I slid the phone back into my pocket and waved my arms out over the pond. "Been a while since we've been here, huh?"

"I still come here sometimes," she said. "It's peaceful and it brings back good memories."

Laura lived close enough to the park to walk. "Yeah? Well, I'm glad you suggested meeting here. It *does* bring back some good times." And it did. I leaned my elbows on the railing and gazed out over the pond. Several turtles sunned themselves on a log in the water.

Laura inched closer to me on the wooden railing, almost touching my elbow. "Remember the time Lizzie accidentally dropped her shoe in the water and Miller jumped right in after it, without even bothering to take off his own shoes? He squished around school for two days, and he smelled like a swamp creature."

"Miller always smells like a swamp creature."

"This is true." Something splashed in the water to our right, and Laura turned to catch a glimpse. She pressed into me, and the sun backlit her, highlighting a few stray strands of her long hair. Part of me wanted to bend over and kiss her. Part of me thought it would be really, really weird bending over and kissing a girl who was like your sister. "What was that? Kermitasaurus, the giant killer frog?"

I laughed. We'd always joked about wildly deformed—and demented—creatures inhabiting the woods. We made up stories about them coming out at night and pillaging the nearby houses, snatching up kids, and eating dogs. That phase hadn't lasted long; as I remember, Miller pounded that one to death until we all got sick and tired of hearing him drone on about nuclear radiation accidents and giant toads with nine legs.

"How's the swimming going?"

Back to my struggles. "I dunno. I've got some kind of mental block or something. I mean, I'm pretty athletic. I'm not a total loser, right?"

"Not totally."

"So how come I can't swim?"

Laura pursed her lips. They weren't as full as Allie's, but they weren't bad. At all. "Maybe you're right, maybe it is something up here." She tapped the side of her head. "Did you have some kind of traumatic experience in the water when you were younger?"

My breath caught. Aside from my mother, I'd never discussed what had happened to Uncle Steve. Not with Miller, not with anybody. The blood seemed to drain from my face.

Laura must have realized something was up because she touched my arm, concern on her face. "Nick?"

I swallowed. Hard. "As a matter of fact..."

"What?"

I swallowed hard again. "When I was six, my Uncle Steve drowned. And I was there when it happened." I tried to say it matter-of-factly, but my voice cracked a bit.

"Oh my God. I'm sorry," she said. "That must have been horrible."

"Yeah, it was pretty bad." Part of me wanted to spill it all, every last excruciating detail; part of me wasn't sure I could get out the story without breaking down.

Laura paused, letting the idea sink in. "It could be why you're having such a hard time."

I nodded, not trusting my voice to say anything.

"People's minds work in strange ways." Laura spoke in the same gentle tone that Mom did when I needed her love and support. "And just because something terrible happened to your uncle doesn't mean it will happen to you."

I couldn't tell her the complete story, not now. Just couldn't. So I nodded. In my head, I knew she was right. What happened to Uncle Steve had no bearing on what would ever happen to me. In my heart, all I could feel now was the terror—and guilt—I felt then as I peered over the side of the boat after Uncle Steve fell in. I bit the inside of my lip and focused on Laura's face, trying to put the past behind me.

"I think you're doing a brave thing," she said. "Learning to swim, after what happened."

I threw my hands up. "Except I can't swim. I just can't. And I'll never learn. Who freaking cares?"

Laura placed her hand on my shoulder. "Nick. Chill. You'll figure it all out. In fact, someday, I bet you'll look back on this whole thing and find it funny."

"Ha ha," I said in a monotone.

"Just try not to think about the fact you can't swim, and why you can't swim, and if you'll ever be able to swim. Next time you're at the pool, just be in the moment, clear your mind, and try to be one with the water."

"Since when did you become a Buddhist?"

"Just call me Zen Master Laura." She closed her eyes, touched her forefingers to her thumbs, and began chanting "ohmmmm." After ten seconds, she busted out laughing and her eyes sprang open. "Come on, you know I'm right. You need to relax."

I laughed too. "Yeah, maybe you're right."

"No maybes about it. I'm *always* right." She turned serious and started twirling a strand of hair around her fingers. "Listen..."

"What?"

"Bethany's having a party Friday night, and I was wondering if you wanted to go." The words spilled out of her mouth. She glanced at me, and there was something in her face, something I didn't recall seeing before. And I'm pretty sure I would have remembered something like that.

"I...uh...oh, crap. I'm going away on Friday." *To a stupid mountain cabin with my mom and her stupid boyfriend.* "Sorry."

Laura's face seemed to deflate. "Oh. Too bad. Well, there'll be other parties, right?" She swung back around and gazed out over the pond.

"Sure." Had Laura asked me here just to invite me to the party? "I'd rather go to the party, but my mom and her boy—"

She cut me off with a wave of her hand. "Hey, no sweat, Nick. I'm sure you'll have fun. We can hang out when you get back."

"Sounds fun. We can hit the mall or something. You, me, Miller. Johnny B might be around, too. We can call it, 'The Three Amigos—and

Miller—Storm the Mall.'"

"Si, the three amigos." Laura's face seemed to turn a chalky gray, as if she were about to lose her lunch.

"Great," I said, still thinking about Laura inviting me to the party.

"Yeah, great." Her tone said *not great.*

Although there had been plenty of times I'd bugged the crap out of girls, I couldn't remember ever disappointing a girl before, at least not like that. Laura and I stood on the dock, side-by-side, watching a squadron of dragonflies flutter around in formation. In the background, we could hear birds in the trees, chirping their little hearts away. After a few minutes, Laura said she had to go, and I watched her walk off with a weird churning in my gut.

Weird, but kinda good, too.

Chapter Twelve: T-minus 9 days

Time to Man Up

The next day, Miller practically begged to come to the pool with me while I practiced. He said he wanted someplace serene to read, but I knew better. He wanted to scope out the hot chicks again from behind his mirrored shades. I thought about pointing out he didn't even have a book or magazine with him, but let it slide.

Johnny B—fresh from band camp—joined us. We snagged three chaise lounges by the deep end, near the diving well, where we had a good view of the entire pool—and more important, an unobstructed view of the prime sunbathing area. It was right after lunch, and the pool would be filling up soon.

"Man, you should have seen some of those geeks. Goofy looking, talking about some kind of crazy Japanese card game. Like Super Double Pokemon or something." Johnny B was spreading sunscreen on his ghost-white body. And he had a long body. He was about six-four, not even counting three inches of bright orange hair. Unfortunately, he was as skinny as a Styrofoam pool noodle. *Who* was the goofy-looking geek?

"I heard about that game," Miller said, not surprisingly. He seemed to gravitate to the latest trends, no matter what country they originated in. Fashion trends were another story. Today, he wore some kind of straw thingy on his head. I guess his grandmother had reclaimed her floppy hat.

Johnny B eyed him as he slathered some of the white cream on his narrow chest. "At least there were a few nice-looking girls."

"Did you get anything?" Miller asked.

"A gentleman doesn't tell."

"So you struck out. Figures," Miller said. "What do you expect? You went to *band camp*."

"It's better than it sounds." Johnny B looked at me for support. "Really."

I just shrugged. It couldn't be much worse than it sounded.

Miller snapped his fingers twice. "Heads up."

PZ stalked toward us in her lopsided way. Her mouth was a horizontal slash below angry eyes. Hell, we hadn't even done anything yet. She aimed toward us like a heat-seeking missile. "Boys." She shook a finger at us, as if she were scolding a dog. "You must be quiet today. Our members and their guests deserve much obedience, no?"

Miller pretended to cough, and Johnny B cleared his throat. I nodded and bit my cheek, trying to keep a straight face, always a challenge around PZ. Even though she'd been in this country longer than I'd been alive, she still hadn't conquered the language. Of course, if I ever moved to Farawayistan, I'd probably mangle things, too.

"You are laughing at me?" PZ squinted at us, and her entire face wrinkled under the pressure.

"No, ma'am. We'll be quiet. We have much obedience for everyone here," Miller said. Johnny B snorted, then turned it into another throat clearing.

PZ's glare intensified. She shook her finger more forcefully. "I can have you thrown from the pool if you do not listen."

We hadn't done anything at all. Why was it that three teenage boys always were presumed guilty? "We won't cause anyone any problems. Promise."

"You had better not be cause problems." She sneered and shuffled off. As she headed back to the pool office, she didn't stop to harass anyone else, including a bunch of younger kids squirting water pistols at each other near the baby pool.

"Man. She's too old to have PMS, right?" Miller asked.

"Ignore her," I said. "She's harmless."

"Yeah, like a landmine is harmless. Nothing, then one wrong step and blammo," Miller said.

"So, watch your step around her," I said.

"Hey, you learn how to swim yet?" Johnny B was still smearing sunscreen on his body. He'd moved south, massaging it into his hairless legs.

"Working on it."

Miller chimed in. "Forget it. He's hopeless. He's going to be tooling around on his bike and begging rides off us." He pointed at me. "You're paying for the gas, dude."

Johnny B worked the cream between his toes. "I have a cousin who can't swim."

"Really?" I asked.

"Really," he said. "Of course, she's only three months old." Johnny B and Miller broke into a laughing fit, only to have it end when Miller started coughing up a lung.

"Sometimes I have that effect on people," Johnny B said, still chuckling over his lame joke.

"Yeah, well...I'll learn," I said.

Miller coughed a final time. "Guess who his swimming instructor is?"

"Uh—" Johnny B began.

"Allie Merskie," Miller said, checking out the pool deck to make sure she wasn't standing nearby. Of course, he'd been checking out the pool deck for Allie since we'd arrived about half an hour ago.

"No shit. Well, that ought to inspire you. Don't want to look like a total dork in front of her." Johnny B closed the tube of sunscreen and wiped his hands on the tops of his thighs.

"Too late," Miller said. "But Nick probably doesn't care too much about what Allie thinks of him."

"Why not?" Johnny B asked.

I wanted to ask "why not?" too, but kept my mouth shut.

"Because Laura's got the hots for our boy here." Miller reached over and tried to grab my arm, but I leaned back out of the way.

Johnny B laughed. "Get real. She's one of the gang. We've known her since third grade."

Actually, since first grade. But rather than correct him, I kept quiet, hoping this whole topic of discussion would blow over like a fast-moving storm cloud.

Miller held up three fingers in a scout's pledge. "Truth. I saw it with my own two eyes. At the mall, here at the pool. She wants him. Big time."

Johnny B stared at me. "What do you have to say for yourself? Is it true?"

"What? Laura? Naw. Like you said, she's one of us." I pretended to shiver. "Come on, that would be too weird." I thought back to my feelings at the pond. What would the guys think about that? Would they believe I made up the whole thing? Had I imagined Laura's hidden intent?

"You should totally do her," Miller said. "I would if I had the chance."

Lightning quick, Johnny B jabbed Miller in the shoulder with his fist. "Shut up. Don't be a dick."

I punched Miller in the other shoulder. "Yeah, what he said."

"Ow, shit." Miller took off his cap and tried to swat Johnny B but didn't come close. Even though he was skinny, Johnny B was stronger than he looked. And those long arms had quite a reach. "I'm not making this up. I can tell things like that. As strange as it may seem, Laura is attracted to Mr. Carlin."

Johnny B cocked his head at me, but didn't say anything else about Laura. I breathed easier as the storm cloud drifted off.

A couple girls we didn't know walked by, and Miller tracked them as they found seats on the other side of the diving well. Seconds later, they shimmied out of their cover-ups and spread out their colorful beach towels. "I love summer," Miller said. "I need to come to the pool more often."

I hoped Laura also would make an appearance here today. I'd been thinking a lot about our conversation at the pond yesterday, about things I could have said. Funny how you always thought of the good lines hours after the conversation ended.

"Hey, you going to the party on Friday night?" Johnny B asked.

Miller sat up. "What? What party?"

"At Bethany's. You didn't hear about it?"

"No. I did not." Miller turned to me. "Did you know about the party?"

"I maybe heard something about it," I said.

"Who told you?" Miller asked.

"Uh, Laura said something about it." I noticed Johnny B's right eyebrow inch up.

"Well, how come nobody told me?" Miller was doing that thing with his lips—his wounded guy expression.

"Stow it, Miller. I'm telling you now," Johnny B said. "You guys going?"

"Can't. I'm going away for the weekend."

"The beach?" Johnny B asked.

"I wish. We're going to some resort in West Virginia."

"Watch out for cannibals," Miller said. "And worse, watch out for inbreds." He hummed the beginning of the song from the movie *Deliverance*, which we'd seen on Netflix a few weeks ago. I didn't see the need to tell him that the movie actually took place in Georgia.

"My mom's boyfriend is coming." I could use a little sympathy, even from my two loser friends.

"So?" Johnny B stretched his arms, and his armpits were even whiter than the rest of him, if that were possible.

"So? So, how would you feel if you went on vacation, and your mom spent the whole time holding hands with some guy?"

Johnny B shrugged. "Like I always feel when I go on vacation with my parents."

"At least that guy is your dad," I said.

"Well, I *wish* my mom and dad hung out together on vacation. Then I could go off and do what I wanted," Miller said. "Instead, my mom hovers over me like she's my personal bodyguard. Hah, personal nag is more like it."

"Jason's only twelve years older than us. It's downright creepy thinking about him and my mom…" I shivered, this time for real. It was creepy. I tried not to let my mind wander in that direction, but…

"I thought you were cool with him. Didn't he take you out driving one day?" Miller asked.

"He did, but… I don't know. I guess he's okay." Of course, my mom deserved better than *okay*. She deserved the best. "I'm going in."

I left Miller and Johnny B to work on their tans and hopped into the pool.

The cold water snapped me to attention. I fixed the goggles over my eyes, ducked my head under to get my hair wet, then slicked it back out of my way. I half dog paddled, half walked over to a semi-clear spot near a wall so I could practice without smacking into anyone.

I stretched my muscles and sank until my chin bobbed at the water line. Closed my eyes. Tried to follow Laura's advice and forget about why I couldn't swim. Forget about the past and Uncle Steve and my dozens of swimming lessons with all those different instructors. I put thoughts of the swimming test and driving and Allie and Laura and Jason out of my mind. I was in the *now*.

I took a few deep breaths and visualized myself swimming across the pool. Arms stroking effortlessly through the clear water, legs kicking up a wake of white. My head swiveling to the side as I took a breath. Bubbles flowing in a tight stream from my mouth underwater. In my mind's eye, all I saw was Nick Carlin cutting through the pool like Michael Phelps.

I'd become one with the chlorinated water.

After a final deep breath, I pushed off from the wall and held myself in a streamlined pose. Then I started stroking. Right, pull down the water, left, pull down the water. Kick, kick, kick. I glided through the water like a fish. My confidence rose. I could do this. I could swim.

I kept going, Stroke, stroke, stroke. Kick, kick, kick. Mid-stroke, a jolt of panic hit me. I'd been forgetting to breathe! I blew out the air through my mouth, all at once, then turned my head, gulping for air. My arms broke down, and my kicking petered out to a few uncoordinated top-of-the foot slaps. Water gushed into my mouth and up my nose, and I cut all engines. Shit and double shit.

I might have become one with the water, but I still couldn't swim. So much for Laura's great advice. I pulled off my goggles and scanned the pool deck, hoping to spot the Zen Master herself.

No luck. I guess she had better things to do than hang out with an uncoordinated loser.

Chapter Thirteen: T-minus 8 days

Two Words: Fo-Cus!

I had my lesson with Allie on Friday, and although she said I was making progress, I figured she was just trying to make me feel better. She told me to practice over the weekend, and we'd keep on going next week. She seemed so positive and encouraging about me actually learning how to swim, I didn't have the heart to tell her I'd almost given up all hope.

On the bright side, she said her parents were impressed with how my tutoring went with Colin and wanted to book me for more sessions. Maybe even twice-a-week, if things went well. I wasn't sure how her parents got their information, but I was willing to work with Colin. I mean, thirty bucks an hour is thirty bucks an hour, no matter how rude the student.

After the swim lesson, I'd trudged home, not in the mood to get together with anyone. We were leaving that evening for our little vacation in the woods, and no matter how I tried to spin it to myself, I didn't see much chance of having a good time. I spent about ten minutes digging through junk in the back of my closet, trying to find something I could bring along that would take my mind off the impending agony. No luck. I guess I could always take some of Mom's vermin traps and see what I could catch in the woods.

The clock on my wall read 4:30. Only a couple hours before we loaded up and moved out. But I hadn't even packed yet. My mind kept returning to my visit to the pond the other day and, more specifically, Laura. In all the years I'd known her, I'd always considered her just one of the group. Sure, she smelled a lot nicer than any of the guys, but I never had any feelings for her. Even though Miller was pretty much on target with his "sex thoughts every five seconds" theory, Laura had never been part of them. At least not until recently. Now I thought about Laura constantly. Or Allie. Sometimes I even thought about both of them together.

But what to do about it?

Of course, if I wasn't leaving town, I could have pursued things with Laura at Bethany's party. A disturbing thought entered my mind. Maybe Laura would meet someone tonight and fall madly in love with him. They'd go out a few times, continue to hit it off, and they'd be an item all the way through the last two years of high school while I hung out with Miller and Johnny B, *talking* about meeting girls, instead of *actually* meeting girls.

The same question knocked again, this time louder. What could I do about it? I was going to spend the next two and a half days in the wilderness. I cursed Jason for the hundredth time. If not for him, I'm pretty sure we wouldn't be going on this torture-trip. Figures that my mom's love life would get in the way of mine. Hers was tons better than my nonexistent one.

What could I do about Laura? I lay on my bed, staring at the ceiling. Slowly, an answer to my problem gelled. It was kinda lame, but it would probably do the trick. I pulled the blanket up over myself and waited for Mom to come home from work.

* * *

I only had to wait about thirty minutes before I heard the front door slam. Then Jason's greetings. A few more minutes, and there was a *knock-knock-knock* on my bedroom door. "Nick-o? You in there?"

I emitted a feeble grunt.

Another *rap-rap*. Sharper. "Nick?"

"Come in." I sounded as weak as I could.

Mom pushed the door open. My lamp was off, but some light leaked into the room around the edges of the curtains. "Hi, Ma," I managed.

"Oh my, what's the matter?" She took a few steps into the room. "You don't sound too good."

I sighed.

"What's wrong?" She slowly approached my bed, as if she were afraid something would come jumping out at her. Maybe it was her pest control training.

"Don't feel well," I croaked.

She lowered herself onto the bed next to me and immediately shot her hand over my forehead. "Hmm. You don't feel warm. What hurts?"

I went over what I'd prepared. Didn't want to lay it on too thick. I raised my head a few inches. "Stomach aches. Headaches. Feel kinda weak all over." My head fell back to the pillow.

"Oh, Nick-o. I'm so sorry." She gently squeezed my arm. "Have you eaten? Can I get you something?"

I grunted. "No. Don't think I can hold anything down."

Mom sat on the bed, shaking her head.

"I'm sorry," I whispered.

Mom looked down at me, and I couldn't read her expression like I normally could. It was shadowy in the room, but there was something else. Maybe she'd seen right through me and was thinking up a good punishment.

"Just get better, huh?"

Relief surged through me. "Sure, Mom. I'll try. I guess we'll all have to go away a different weekend, huh?"

"Don't worry about that, okay?"

I put some perk in my voice. "Hey, why don't you and Jason go away, just like you planned? I'll be all right here by myself."

"But you're sick, Nick-o."

She stared at me some more, this time her expression reflected the pain of seeing someone you loved—me—suffer. I hated making her feel bad, but...sometimes you gotta do what you gotta do. "I'll be all right. Really."

"What kind of mother would I be if I left you here alone? A terrible one, that's what kind."

"Mom. You know what I'm like when I'm sick. I just want to be left alone. I'm sure I'll be feeling better tomorrow—at least enough to take care of myself." I reached out for her hand and gave it a reassuring pat. "You and Jason go. Have a great time. I'll be fine, I swear."

She tilted her head at me, like a dog trying to figure out a radio. "I don't know." She chewed on her lip. I almost had her, I could feel it.

"You deserve a little break. You've been working awful hard. I'll be just fine." *Too much?*

She exhaled. "Why don't we see how you are in the morning? Then we can decide what to do?"

Crap. On to Plan B.

* * *

I watched the numbers on my alarm clock march by, the slowest march in history. Finally, after what seemed like about thirty hours, the numbers crept from 9:59 to 10:00. I slipped out of bed and got dressed without turning on a light. Didn't want to risk even a faint glow appearing under my door. All I needed was for Mom to see my light on, figure I was awake, and come investigate.

I wasn't too worried about Mom poking her head in and finding me gone. She usually went to bed pretty early, and she hadn't really checked on me at night since I'd started high school. Especially when I had the door closed, which was pretty much all the time. And I knew she wouldn't knock, not wanting to wake up her sick kid.

I moved to the window but paused.

What if she *did* want to check on her sick kid? I gathered up a bunch of clothes and threw them on the bed, then pulled the blanket up over where my head should be.

I dug around in my closet like a blind man, searching for an old metal flashlight I remembered seeing during my earlier excavation project. Finally, my fingers closed around the cool cylinder, and I flicked it on, holding my hand around the bulb end to dim the light. I stood by the door and played the beam on the bed, trying to duplicate what Mom might see if she happened to check on me. It looked like the form of a boy sleeping peacefully. A sick boy. Perfect.

Satisfied with my ruse, I tossed the flashlight back into the closet and moved to my escape route, the window. Using the heels of my palms on the window frame, I gently worked it open slowly, very slowly, so it wouldn't squeak or scrape. I'd ducked out a few other times in the past couple years. I'd told her the window had been painted shut, and I was pretty sure she believed me. Since I never got yelled at, I'm guessing she never even knew about my nighttime excursions.

The night air wasn't much cooler than the day air. Hot and heavy. The contrast with the air conditioning made it seem even hotter. I squeezed through the window out onto the roof covering the screened porch. I shut the window behind me, again going slowly to prevent any telltale screeching. Duckwalking, I made my way to the corner of the roof. The porch roof below was much flatter than the regular roof, so I wasn't worried about losing my balance and killing myself. Besides, it was only about ten feet down to the back yard. If I fell, at most I'd break my arm. Well worth the risk.

When I reached the corner, I glanced back at my window, half expecting to see Mom's face staring at me. But all the windows were dark, including her bedroom window down at the other end of the house.

Now came the trickiest part of my escape. Finding the first foothold along the side of the screened porch. Whoever built the porch had decided to add some design flourishes. The original owner had set a series of horizontal wooden panels into the outer wall. In my opinion, it looked pretty crappy, but I was thankful. It provided me with a ready-made ladder. After the first time I'd snuck out and practically killed myself on a loose board, I'd gone to work one day when Mom was out and reinforced the shaky planks with some big-ass nails. Now it was sturdy enough to support Miller, if he ever came along with me.

I flattened myself on the roof and scooched backward, dangling my legs down. With my right foot, I searched for the first rung of my ladder. I needed to be careful, or I was liable to put a hole in the screen, and I'd have a hard time explaining that. Panic was about to set in, but finally my toes hit something hard. I eased myself off the roof and made my way down, lightly holding on to the drainspout to help keep my balance.

My feet hit terra firma. The backyard was dark; only a little light spilled over from a porchlight Mrs. Hangoddy always kept on beside her back door.

I finally exhaled. Success.

A voice came from the darkness behind me. "Feeling better, Nick?"

Chapter Fourteen

I whirled around. Jason leaned against the outer porch door. He took a puff from his cigarette, tilted his head back, and exhaled into the night air.

"I...uh." I didn't move, shocked by the sight of Jason. I'd been so close...

"Well, I'm glad you seem to be doing better. I know your mother will be relieved." Moonlight reflected off Jason's face, and I thought I detected a little smirk. That would be a safe guess—Jason usually had a smirk on his face.

"Yeah, I am feeling a little better. Thanks for asking." I debated what to say. Give an excuse or come clean and throw myself on the mercy of Jason?

He took another long drag. "Nice night, eh?"

"I guess."

"Summer's my favorite season. Warm weather, long days. Things seem more relaxed, too, you know?"

"Yeah." I didn't feel very relaxed right now.

"Since you seem to be feeling better, I suppose we'll be leaving in the morning. To the resort." He flicked some ash onto the ground.

"I suppose." Unless Mom's punishment crippled me somehow.

With his cigarette hand, Jason gestured out toward the darkness beyond the backyard. "Where you headed?"

Decision time. Tell the truth or spread some B.S.? "I...uh..." I swallowed and tried to read him. Unfortunately, I didn't know him well enough to even speculate what might be running through his mind. "There's this party."

He clicked his tongue. "I remember when I was your age. There was always a party somewhere."

"Yeah."

"You don't want to go on vacation with us, do you?"

I was about to tell him he was wrong, but he didn't give me a chance.

"I should say you don't want to go on vacation with *me*." He dropped his cigarette and stubbed it out with his flip-flop. "I get it, Nick. It's been just you and your mom for a long time. Hell, forever. Now I'm intruding, like some cockroach in one of your mom's customer's kitchen cabinets."

I shook my head. I didn't think he was exactly as bad as a cockroach. "I wouldn't say that."

Jason laughed. "It's okay. I'd probably feel the same way if I were in your shoes."

No response from me.

"There a girl involved?" he asked.

"A girl?"

"At the party. Is there some girl you're after?"

My face flushed. Luckily, it was too dark for Jason to see. I think. "Sort of."

"There usually is. Well, you know how you feel about that girl? That's how I feel about your mom. Keep that in mind." He continued to lean against the porch door.

I nodded, then realized he might not be able to see my head bob in the darkness. "Sure, I understand."

"Good. Long as we're straight."

Silence passed between us for a minute. I knew I should go in the house and watch TV or something, but I just stood there. He wasn't my father. He couldn't force me to go back inside. A few drops of sweat trickled down the back of my neck. "So…"

"So?" Jason echoed back.

I didn't answer him right away, trying to guess how this would play out. I had trouble coming up with a scenario that would end well for me.

"So?" Jason said again. "You want to know what I'm going to tell your mom?"

He'd tell Mom he caught me sneaking out, and she'd punish me. Ground me, probably. This was going to be worth a week or two, at the least. Just enough to wreck my summer. Shit. "No. It doesn't really matter what you tell her. She won't be happy." My shoulders sagged.

Jason laughed. "No, she wouldn't be."

Wouldn't be? Not "won't be." My pulse quickened, and I stood straight. "You're not going to tell her?"

"Nah. Like I said, I remember when I was your age. You're not going to do anything bad, right? You're just chasing some tail. No harm in that. In fact, I'd say you were doing our gender proud." He pushed himself off the side of the door. "I think I'm going to turn in. Listen, don't stay out too late. We'll be heading out early in the morning to the resort—all three of us. You can tell your mother you had a miraculous recovery and would love to go on a little vacation." He opened the door to the porch. "Oh, Nick, do me a favor?"

My pulse still pounded in my ears. "Sure. Anything." I figured I owed him, big-time.

"When you get back, try coming in through the door. I wouldn't want you to get hurt falling off the roof, okay?" He chuckled to himself as he went inside.

I exhaled and thanked him silently as I set off for the party.

* * *

I'd known Bethany Hempstead for a long time. All the way through elementary school we'd ridden the same bus, had most of the same teachers, bumped into each other at the grocery store or at the mall. But up until a couple of years ago, we'd never said more than thirty words to each other at one time. Part of it had been my shyness, and part of it had been that I'd always been intimidated by her. She'd been the smartest and most popular girl at Fox Creek Elementary, a position she also held at Chantilly Middle. Unfortunately for her, the competition in high school was much tougher, and she'd been knocked down a peg or two. In fact, she'd been knocked down so far she'd actually talked to me a few times lately. Although both of us being pals with Laura may have had something to do with it.

Bethany lived only a mile away, and it took me about ten or fifteen minutes to jog over there. The Hempsteads' huge house sat well off the main street, and their long driveway sloped upward and wound through a manicured lawn. Large trees bordered the drive, allowing only a faint glimmer of moonlight to filter through.

I slowed to a walk as I climbed the drive, allowing my heart rate to return to normal. As soon as the house came into view, the trees on either side gave way to old-fashioned lampposts with fake, flickering flames. Closer to the house, a homemade sign on a stake had an arrow pointing around the side with the words, "Around Back" written on it in big bold Sharpie letters.

I'd been to Bethany's for a party last year and remembered how cool her backyard was. A little grotto next to a pool. A barbecue pit. A waterfall down a slope of rocks feeding one side of the pool. A meandering path circling the entire yard shielded by walls of plants. Plenty of places to get a little privacy while still enjoying the party atmosphere.

Finding Laura was job one.

I swung open the back gate and followed a short path beside the house toward party sounds—music and laughter. Tiki torches had been set up at intervals, and groups of people dotted the humongous back patio. Two metal washtubs full of drinks flanked the back door. I nodded to a few kids as I walked over to get something. The icy tubs contained soda, but I knew there were plenty of hidden flasks around. These parties usually adhered to a "Don't ask, don't tell, don't pass out" guideline. I grabbed a Sprite from the closest tub and wiped my cold, wet hand on my shirt.

I stood there for a moment, trying to scope out the party without looking too obvious. I thought I recognized a few guys from Mrs. Ratner's English class, but I needed to keep my focus. I didn't care about shooting the shit with them; I cared about finding out where things stood with Laura and me.

The pool was full. Bethany was at one end, hanging on one of those floaty chairs surrounded by four or five guys, all splashing and showing off their six-pack abs. Another bunch of guys played water basketball at the other end of the pool. A cluster of kids sat in a circle of plastic chairs on the far side of the slate patio.

No sign of Laura. I was about to do a reconnaissance run—a lap around the backyard path—when Zach Worth and his posse stomped down the stairs from the two-tiered deck that overlooked the whole yard. I thought about backing up quickly and disappearing into the shadows by the wall, but he'd spotted me.

"Hey, if it isn't Bugboy." He had a can of Coke in his hand. Judging from the smell on his breath, he'd spiked it with something.

"Hey, Zach. How's it going?" I tried to keep my voice from warbling.

"Outstanding. Truly outstanding." He grinned at me like he knew the punchline of a joke I'd never heard.

"That's good, I guess." I glanced over his shoulder, plotting my escape route. All I needed was a crack, and I'd be gone.

"Yes, it is, Buggy." He narrowed his eyes. "Are you crashing this party? 'Cause if you are, that's not cool. In fact, we'd…" He gestured to his boys behind him. "Well, we'd have to escort you out."

"I was invited."

Zach's eyebrows jumped. "Really? Bethany invited you?"

"Uh, sure. I know Bethany. We went to second grade together."

"Second grade?" Zach cackled. "You guys play dolls together? Second grade?" He stepped closer, into my space, into my *face*. "That was a few years ago, dude. Did Bethany herself invite you? Sometime after puberty, I mean?" Zach's buddies thought he was hysterical, and they started bumping fists with each other.

Zach stared at me, and I got the feeling he was deciding if he should flex his muscles and pound me into a paste or let me pass. He took a swig from his can of Coke and whatever.

"Actually, Laura invited—"

"Hey boys, excuse me a sec." A man—presumably Bethany's father— came up behind Zach carrying an armful of sodas. As he bent over to dump them into one of the tubs, half a dozen rolled out of his arms and tumbled to the ground. One can burst open, sending sticky spray everywhere, while the others bounced and rolled and skittered away.

Zach and his friends bent over to help retrieve them, while I seized my opening and skirted the whole mess to freedom. I didn't look back.

I gave the pool a wide berth and located the beginning of the walkway that circled the yard. I passed under a metal arch with ivy growing on it and found myself on a narrow dirt-and-gravel path. Tiki torches lit the way, and vines and bushes grabbed at me as I went along. Every so often, the path would widen into a little alcove, which afforded a touch of privacy. Some even had little chairs and benches. The parents probably put them in for reflection. The teenagers used them for *affection*.

The first alcove I passed was occupied by a couple kissing so intently they didn't even open their eyes as I scuffed by. The second secluded spot I came to hid another couple, holding hands and inspecting some of the abundant foliage. I got the feeling they'd been inspecting something else until they heard me approach. I didn't know any of those kids, but they looked like they were having a fine time at the party.

As I rounded a bend in the path, I noticed a shock of red hair above a holly, like the star on a Christmas tree. Johnny B. Had he managed to persuade some girl to take a walk with him? Two more steps and I had my answer—of course not. Miller stood by his side, gesturing wildly and talking a mile a minute. When he saw me, he stopped in mid-sentence and pointed. "Hey, Nicky, you made it." He held up his hands like a cop stopping traffic. "Wait, wait. Don't tell me. Your mom and that guy broke up."

"No such luck."

"So what happened? Mom had to flush a family of bats out of some lady's belfry?" Johnny B asked. For some reason, he was fascinated by Mom's job.

"No. Snuck out."

"Nice going, Nick. We'll make a man out of you yet," Miller said. Both guys held out their fists for a bump. I kept my fist to myself.

"Oh, did you sneak out too?" I asked.

"Nope," he said, sheepish grin on his face.

"Hell, his mom even dropped him off and is going to pick him up," Johnny B said. The way he said it made me wonder if Johnny B would have preferred to be at the party without Miller shadowing his every move.

"Eff you, storkman," Miller said.

Johnny B rolled his eyes and waved him off. "Did you just get here?" he asked me.

"Yeah. Gave the slip to Zach over by the sodas and decided to do the circuit." I left out the part about searching for Laura. "Who else is here?"

"The usual suspects," Miller said, breaking out a smirk. "And your girlfriend is about twenty yards up the path." He paused for a moment, solely for dramatic effect. "With Air Force."

Johnny B swatted Miller. "Not cool." Then he looked at me and shrugged. "But he is right."

Air Force was Harmon Freedlander III, a guy who transferred into school last year from someplace in Colorado. All he talked about was how he was going to go to the Air Force Academy and fly fighters for a living, like his father and grandfather. He bragged he'd seen the movie *Top Gun* fifty times and knew every one of Tom Cruise's lines by heart. Unfortunately for me, he was also blond, about six-two, and made of hardened metal, just like the planes he wanted to fly. He'd never expressed much interest in girls, beyond calling every plane "she or her" as in, "I'll take her to ten thousand feet and roll her over and spank her like a virgin." Or some such nonsense.

"Oh, Nicky boy. Wake up, Nick." Miller snapped his fingers in front of my face. "You with us?"

"What? Yeah, sure."

"Aren't you going to do something about it?" Miller asked.

"About what?"

"About your girlfriend off in the bushes with a guy who is clearly not you," Miller said. Next to him, Johnny B sort of nodded, sort of shrugged.

"I don't care. Laura is not my girlfriend," I said.

Now Johnny B spoke. "I can see your wooden nose growing, Pi-Nick-io."

"That's not all the wood that grows when we mention Laura," Miller added.

Johnny B jerked his thumb up the path. "That way. Maybe you should go say hi, or something."

"Promise me that if you're planning on throwing down with him, you'll let me know. I love fights," Miller said.

My mouth went dry. Did I want to barge in on Laura and Air Force? What if I found them in a compromising situation? I could make it look like an accident. Just strolling through, and, why, look who it is. My heart thump-thumped in my chest.

Johnny B hooked his thumb again. "Go ahead. What have you got to lose? Besides your dignity, your self-respect, and your pride?"

My lunch?

"Don't be a chickenshit. You can't let a geek like Air Force make the moves on Laura. She's our friend," Johnny B said.

I nodded and opened my mouth to ask why they hadn't done anything, but all the cotton in there prevented any words from coming out. I took a big gulp of my Sprite. "Yeah, right. She's our friend. Maybe we all should go over there."

I started up the path, but Johnny B and Miller didn't budge. "Maybe just you should," Johnny B said. "Yell if you need backup." They both stared at me. I was in this alone. Man or mouse?

I made my decision. I'd faked being sick, lied to my mother, snuck out of the house, now owed Jason. If I didn't do what I'd come here for, Miller was right. I was a chickenshit, supersized. "Okay, gents. Wish me luck."

"Godspeed," Johnny B said as he put two fingers over his chest.

"Go get 'em, tiger," Miller said. "Grrrr."

I saluted them, turned, and trudged down the path, mentally preparing my surprised reaction. *Oh, Laura, hi. Small world, eh?* Nope, too hokey. *Hey Laura, there you are. I've been searching for you.* Too stalkerish. *What's shakin', babe? Wanna hook up?* Way too...Miller-ish.

After zigzagging down the path a bit, I felt a weird rush. A racing heart and a hitch in my breath caused me to stop. I gulped some air and bent over at the hips. In a moment, the physical symptoms subsided, but the discomfort travelled to my head. Maybe I should turn around and seek refuge with Johnny B and Miller and we could argue about the best weapons in Call of Duty. Better yet, I could go back home, pack up some things, and run away. No awkward moments with Laura, no competition with Air Force, no stupid vacation with the soon-to-be stepdad, and no learning to swim. I could hit the road, move in with some nice family in Iowa, and grow corn for a living.

As I stood in the path, hunched over and still a little short of breath, I heard scuffling noises ahead. I barely had time to stand tall and run a hand through my hair before Laura appeared, followed closely—way *too* closely—by Air Force.

When she saw me, she stopped, almost skidding to a halt on the mulch-covered path. "Nick! What are you doing…" Her head moved to her side, and she washed some of the excitement out of her voice. "I thought you were going away this weekend."

Air Force inched up from his position behind until he stood shoulder-to-shoulder with her, although it was more like shoulder-to-head. "Hey, Carlin."

I tipped my chin down at Air Force, the kind of greeting you reserved for acquaintances, not friends. "Hey."

"Nick, I thought you were…" Laura said. When she first saw me, she seemed glad to be looking at my face. Now, she seemed…kinda pissed, although she still had a smile on her face. Maybe it was the fire in the eyes that clued me in. She turned to Air Force. "Harmon, would you mind getting me something to drink. A Coke or something?"

Air Force's jaw rippled, and his nostrils twitched. He glared at me for a second. "Uh, sure. I'm thirsty too. Be right back." Without asking me if I wanted a drink, he touched Laura on her bare shoulder—she looked stunning in a sleeveless yellow shirt—and stomped off. I made a mental note not to get on Air Force's bad side. Or at least not to provoke him any further.

As soon as he was gone, Laura's smile faded. Now she looked pissed off, one hundred percent. "Didn't want to be seen with me?"

"No, that's not it at—"

"Save it for someone who cares. Listen, you don't have to lie to protect me. I'm not your little sister, you know. It's not like I was asking you on a date or anything." She paused and stared right into my pupils, challenging me, goading me, trying to send some kind of message, I think. I wish I understood girls better to receive it properly.

I held my hands out, palms up in the universal sign of confusion. "I don't know what you're saying exactly. I was going away this weekend." My mouth was getting ahead of my brain a little. "I mean, I am going away. Tomorrow. It's just—"

She stepped closer and lowered her voice. "Nick. You don't have to explain. If we showed up together, I'd just be holding you back. Just as well. Harmon and I are really getting to know each other." Her eyebrows did a tiny dance. "Don't worry about me. He's cool."

Laura and Air Force didn't seem like they fit together. Like peanut butter and cottage cheese. Gross. I lowered my voice, too. "Come on, Laura. Air Force?"

She wrinkled her nose at the nickname. "Harmon's a funny guy. Very entertaining."

Funny? Who was being funny now? "Sure, sure." It came out sounding super-sarcastic and Laura's eyes blazed again. I wanted to say nice things about him, after all I didn't want to further piss off Laura, but...Harmon wasn't right for her, any way you looked at it.

"What? Don't tell me you're jealous, Nicky? We're just amigos, right? Isn't that what you said at the pond?"

"I...uh." My male-mind searched for the right words, those slick words that would make this conversation—and whatever thing Laura and I might have—work out like I wanted. Only problem: I didn't know what I wanted, not exactly.

Laura's gaze shot over my shoulder, and a second later, Harmon elbowed his way around me. "Here you go," he said as he passed Laura a Coke. "I popped it open for you."

I almost gagged.

"Thanks," she said, with extra high-fructose corn syrup in her voice.

Harmon put his arm around Laura's shoulders—those tanned, toned bare shoulders—and glared at me.

I almost gagged again.

Behind me, voices and more scuffling. I turned in time to see Johnny B and Miller crowd into the little clearing in the path. "Hey, hey," Miller said. "Now the party can get started. We're here."

"Hey, Air For...," Johnny B started. "I mean Harmon. How's it hanging?" Everyone knew he said it that way on purpose, and Air Force's glare intensified. I wouldn't have been surprised if Johnny B's clothes caught fire under the heat of the twin phasers.

"It's hanging fine, thank you." Air Force's grip around Laura got tighter, and he flicked his gaze in my direction. I looked off into the upper reaches of the foliage, as if I'd just spotted a howling monkey.

"Good, good," Johnny B replied. "So..."

"So what?" Air Force asked.

"Watcha been doing?" Miller asked, from his usual state of obliviousness.

Laura stepped up. "Just...talking." Her eyes were on me, and I hoped she wouldn't explain what she meant by *talking*, afraid it meant something else besides talking.

I'd had enough. "Well, I think I'm going to circulate. Harmon. Laura. See you later." I didn't bother saying goodbye to Miller and Johnny B. I knew they'd be right on my heels to razz me about Air Force and Laura.

I stayed ahead of them on the path and almost made it out of the backyard before they caught up. "Hey," Johnny B said. "Hold up a sec."

With a sigh, I stopped and turned to face them, square on.

"Can you believe that? Air Force and Laura? Who would have thought?" Miller was all bubbly. "I mean, I could have sworn she was into you!" He jabbed his stubby finger in my direction. "I guess I was wrong, huh?"

I didn't answer, didn't nod, didn't shrug. Just stood there trying to keep it together.

Johnny B slowly shook his head. "Man. Man, oh, man."

"I guess it's just as well, though. Now you can concentrate on trying to nail Allie." Miller snickered, still revved up by it all. "I cannot believe Air Force is making the move on Laura. You know what? I'm pretty sure they weren't just talking, either!"

I remained a statue on the outside. Inside, it was an entirely different story.

Chapter Fifteen: T-minus 7 days

Come On, Dude

"Give me a hand with the bags, will you?" Jason asked. I'd just pulled in front of our cabin, after having driven the two hours from home. Mom never passed up a chance for me to practice driving, and it wasn't often I got some serious highway work, beyond Saturday mornings. My back was a little stiff, but otherwise, I'd handled everything well.

"Sure." I went around to the trunk, removed a couple duffel bags, and set them on the ground. Mom had already gone into the cabin, and I waited for her to come out and tell us the room wasn't acceptable, and she'd get us a new one as soon as she talked to the manager. It was one of those inevitable events, like low tide or the leaves changing colors in autumn.

Jason wrestled Mom's large suitcase out of the trunk, and he wheeled it across the dirt path to the cabin, bumping over roots and branches. Obviously, he hadn't travelled enough with Mom to know her patterns. I suppose in the future, he'd know not to really unpack until the room got Mom's seal of approval.

Mom popped her head out the front door. "The room is perfect. Just perfect," she called out before ducking back in like a prairie dog.

I stood there, not sure what had happened. Had Mom mellowed in her old age? I guess there was a first time for everything. I picked up the duffel bags and toted them inside.

Although the cabin appeared pretty rustic from the outside, we were in a *resort*, so I figured it was all part of the ambiance. Rustic outside like the old days, plush and fancy inside like the modern days. Like at the Wild West place in Disney World.

As soon as I crossed the threshold, I realized the Tree Tops Resort wasn't anything like Disney World. The only oversized mouse I'd see here would be scurrying around in the kitchen. The place smelled moldy, and you could see plywood through the bare spots in the carpet. Multi-colored stains decorated the couch cushions, the drapes hung crookedly—at least on those windows that had drapes—and in one corner, the ceiling dipped precariously low. I guess the owners figured "Tree Tops Dump" wouldn't attract as many customers.

"Hey darling, where do you want this stuff?" Jason asked. He'd gone out and gotten another suitcase and a grocery bag full of something. Food, I hoped. We hadn't passed a McDonald's during the last forty miles of our trip. Or any other fast-food restaurants for that matter.

Mom pointed to one of the two bedrooms. "In there is good. Thanks."

Jason gathered up what he could and hauled it away.

"Nick-o, I'm so glad you're feeling better. Weird, huh? Must have been something you ate."

"Uh, yeah. I guess." Evidently, Jason hadn't narced on me about my sneaking out. Chalk one up in the good-dude column. Although part of me thought he might just be waiting for a better time to get me in trouble. Or maybe he'd hold it over my head as blackmail fodder.

Mom beamed and spun around with her arms outstretched. "Isn't this place charming?"

Had she suffered some kind of stroke or something? Or taken a happy pill? "Mom, this place is kinda..." I made a face as if I'd just smelled a pile of dog crap.

"I think it's kinda cool, myself," Jason said, coming into the room from the bedroom. "Like camping, without having to mess with a tent."

"And with indoor plumbing," Mom added. She put her arm around Jason's waist and squeezed. Even though I'd seen it a hundred times, it still made me a little queasy. "We're going to have a fun time here. I can tell. When was the last time we did something like this, Nick-o?"

Never. We'd never done anything like this. And for good reason. "I thought this was a resort. Not..." I didn't even know how to describe this place, except for *hopeless*.

"It is. It is." She disengaged from Jason and snatched a piece of paper from the *Welcome to The Tree Tops* folder sitting on a desk made entirely of knotty wood. "Here's the activities list. Some stuff you do on your own, like hiking and orienteering. Other stuff, they have classes and workshops. Arts and crafts. Yoga. And they've got plenty of sports, too. Tennis. Rowing. Archery. There's even a horseshoe pit."

This entire place sounded like a horse*shit* pit. And what the heck was orienteering, anyway? Where was the video game arcade? The movie theater? *Any* cool place to hang out and meet other people I could actually *relate* to?

Mom cleared her throat to make sure she had my attention. "There's a pool. You did bring your swim trunks, right, Nick?"

"No, Mom. I guess I'll just have to skinny-dip."

Jason frowned at me, but Mom hadn't heard my wisecrack. She was still preoccupied with the activity sheet in her hand. "Oh, look. There's a trivia contest later this afternoon around the pool. At two-thirty. That sounds like fun."

"Count me in," Jason said.

"What do you say, sport?" Mom asked me.

What do I say? What did I *want* to say? Plenty, but I just shrugged and said, "Sure, why not?" I picked up my duffel bags. "I guess I'll go chill."

I trudged to my room, flopped my bags on the floor, and plopped on the bed. It sagged about a foot, and I settled in the middle of the depression, as if I were lying in a hammock. I pulled my phone out to text Miller. Tell him what a dump this *resort* was. No cell service. Figures. A slow panic grew. I hadn't noticed a TV in the main room, and there certainly wasn't one in here. I bet they didn't have wi-fi either. What was I going to do for two days? Pal around with Mom and her boyfriend? I think I'd prefer to be stranded on a deserted island than have to endure this.

My thoughts were interrupted by a triple rap on the door. Knock, knock, *knock*. Hard, not gentle and caring like my mother's knocks. Before I answered, the door swung open, and Jason stepped in. "Hey, you want to go on a hike?"

I glanced around the room. Bare. My phone didn't work. I didn't pitch horseshoes. I certainly didn't orienteer. At least I didn't *think* I did. I knew how to hike, though. "Sure. Why not?"

We found a trail map in the welcome packet and set off. Mom decided to take a little nap, so it was just me and Jason. After consulting the map, he waved his arm and started walking, making a left out of the short cabin driveway and down the access road toward the forest about thirty yards away. I followed him, keeping about four or five paces behind. He had a faster gait than I did, so every few paces, I'd have to hustle a little to keep up.

At the edge of the trees, Jason paused, checked the map, and then turned to his right. "The trailhead's just down here a bit, I think. Come on, keep up now." A quick glance back at me—to see if I was going to follow him, I guess—and he plowed ahead.

He'd been right. We found the trailhead marked by a small wooden sign: Crow's Mount Trail. Jason turned to me and bumped fists. "Let's do it." Then he spun around and headed down the path.

This path wasn't as level or as manicured as the one around Bethany's back yard, but it *was* covered with mulch and surrounded by foliage. It didn't take much to stir up those feelings I had at the party last night.

The dense forest surrounding the trail was home to hundreds of squirrels and birds and other critters. Did they have relationship problems? Did one squirrel like another squirrel, but then a third squirrel comes along and butts in? Or did the horny little male squirrels just hop on every female squirrel they wanted to? What if Laura and I were squirrels? Or Allie? Were certain squirrels hotter than other squirrels? If you were a squirrel doing the evaluating, I mean?

Almost on cue, two squirrels started chasing each other around the trunk of an oak tree, screeching and skittering. They spiraled up the trunk and out onto some branches, then crossed over to a neighboring tree, chattering the whole way. An odd thought hit me. Was that how adults viewed us as we pursued potential mates? All chatter and chase?

I pictured the way Laura's face drooped the day at the pond when I'd told her I couldn't go to the party with her, then her features slowly morphed into Allie's face, like faces reassembling in some bizarre YouTube video. I heard a game show host's voice, "So, Nick Carlin, it's the moment of choice. Will it be contestant number one, the very sweet Laura DiBennetti, or will it be contestant number two, robo-hottie Allie Merskie?"

I stumbled over a tree root in the trail, took three flailing steps trying to regain my balance, then planted myself, head-first into a pile of dead leaves. I let out a strangled yell and scrambled to my feet before a rogue snake had time to attack. I brushed some forest debris from my shirt.

Jason must have heard me yelp because he turned around, a scowl on his face. He came back down the trail a bit. "You okay?"

Nothing hurt, except my pride. "Yeah. Just, uh, tripped."

"Okay, then. Let's keep going." He didn't move. "Unless you want to turn back."

"I'm fine. Let's go." I didn't feel much like hiking, but there was nothing else to do, and I didn't want Jason to think I was some kind of wuss.

We resumed our trek, and I figured I should concentrate more on my hike and not let my thoughts wander too much. But that's a tall order, because every five seconds…

I willed my mind to think about swimming. I had to learn, absolutely had to. I needed my driver's license. Imagining the shit I'd have to take if I didn't get my license almost made me puke. I mean, six-year-olds could swim! Miller could swim! I bet Air Force could swim ten miles at a time. And I just sank like a horseshoe.

After a while, I lost track of Jason up ahead. But I soldiered on, swatting any branches in my way while doing my best to avoid gnarly tree roots. Sweat had soaked through my t-shirt—under my arms, around the collar, on my belly, and the mosquitoes were enjoying an all-you-can-eat buffet on my neck.

I had my head down, avoiding tree roots, when I almost passed Jason. He sat on a wide, flat rock five yards off the trail.

"Well, you finally made it," he said. A shaft of light penetrated the tree cover and cut a swath across his legs. "How you holding up?"

"Okay."

"Take a load off." Jason moved over on the rock. He didn't look like he'd been sweating at all. In fact, he looked relaxed, like he'd just woken up from a nice nap in an air-conditioned bedroom.

I sat next to him and the rock felt cool on my legs and my butt, even through my shorts. Now the shaft of light cut across my chest.

"I like the woods. Peaceful." He'd picked up a little stick and was drawing imaginary shapes on the rock.

"I guess." Too many bugs and roots for my taste, but it was kinda nice to breathe some fresh air and not hear traffic noise.

"How was the party last night? Catch up with that girl?"

"Uh, yeah. Sort of. By the way, thanks for not telling Mom."

He tipped his head. "Sure. Us guys got to stick together, right?"

"Yeah."

"I sense some troubles with this girl you're after. Tell me about it. I've had some experience with the ladies, you know."

I was pretty sure I didn't want to hear about my mom's boyfriend's previous sexual exploits. I was pretty weirded out by the whole Jason-Mom thing as it was. "Thanks, but forget it. I'll figure something out."

"Okay. Whatever you say. I'm here if you need me."

"Thanks." First Miller, now Jason. Did I have a sign on my forehead saying Relationship Advice Needed?

"I will, however, offer up some unsolicited advice. It's free, so you'll get what you pay for." A crooked smile appeared, then turned into a creepy grin. "There are plenty of fish in the pond. And I'll bet there are dozens who wouldn't mind getting caught by your rod." He winked, a big, exaggerated one. "Know what I mean?"

"Uh, thanks," I mumbled, thinking he and Miller might have more in common than I'd first thought. Jesus! My mom was going to marry this guy? I wonder if he acted differently around her. Not like some too-old frat boy.

"Yeah, I wish I'd done more, uh, fishing the pond when I was younger." Jason leaned back on the rock. "I was pretty popular, but, well, I guess I could have been a little more sociable. Seems like you got a lot of friends. That's good."

"I guess." What if I'd actually asked for his opinion? Would we be here for the next two hours?

"Don't waste your youth."

Jason was all of twenty-eight. Did he think marrying my mom would send him over the hill? "Sounds like good advice."

"I'm not as dumb as I look, you know," he said. "You like to hunt?"

I wasn't sure if that was another lame euphemism or if he actually meant hunting animals, so I gave him one of my patented non-committal shrugs.

He squinted at me. "Ever been?"

"Hunting? No, not really."

"Maybe I'll take you sometime. It'd be fun. Just you and me, waiting for a big whitetail to happen by." He held up his arms and sighted down an imaginary rifle. "Then *ka-pow*. Venison for dinner."

Killing a deer sounded horrible. Sometimes I had trouble with what Mom did, and many of her kills were nasty, disease-carrying pests. Not innocent Bambis. "Maybe we should head back now. Mom might be wondering where we are. Plus…" I tapped my wrist. "It's getting close to lunchtime."

Jason rose and slapped dirt off his butt. "Yeah, I could eat, that's for sure. Let's go, champ."

Champ?

Chapter Sixteen

When Jason and I returned from our hike, we found Mom in her swimsuit, re-reading the welcome packet, waiting for us. We changed into our swim trunks, grabbed some beach towels, and the three of us set off to find something to eat. After a few false starts down dead-end paths, we finally found the one leading to the pool area and the adjoining snack bar. Mom and Jason led the way; I followed at a reasonable distance. Not so far behind to get lost, but not close enough to partake of their stupid lovey-dovey chatter. The more I saw them holding hands and giggling and flirting with each other, the more I was convinced Jason was going to pop the question on this trip.

Which would be great for mom, I guessed, but if it happened, I hoped I wasn't within earshot.

We stood in line at the snack bar, and after being told they were out of chicken fingers and popcorn shrimp, I settled for a cheeseburger and fries. Mom and Jason ordered grilled cheese sandwiches and a fruit bowl to share. We ate our gourmet meals at a picnic table covered with something sticky. Maybe the word "resort" had a different meaning in West Virginia.

I sat in silence, concentrating on my cheeseburger and trying to avoid landing my elbows in the stickiness, while Mom and Jason prattled on about who knows what, oblivious to me. Hell, from the way they touched and made eyes at each other in public, you'd think they were oblivious to everyone.

I finished first and crumpled up my trash, pitching it into a nearby trashcan from fifteen feet. "I'm heading over to the pool."

Mom barely nodded in my direction, and Jason made no acknowledgement whatsoever. He just stabbed a piece of watermelon with his little white plastic fork and popped it into his mouth. Then he leaned over and wiped a smidge of cheese from Mom's chin.

I draped my towel over my shoulder, grabbed Mom's tote bag, and stomped off.

The entrance to the pool wasn't hard to find; I just followed a family of five carrying about three tons of pool stuff. Towels, noodles, an inflatable sea serpent, a plastic bag with a pair of bright red boxers spilling out of it. Two of the kids had white globs of sunscreen on their noses. From the look of things, they were planning to spend quite a lot of time at the pool. Probably because there wasn't anything else to do at this crummy place.

Of course, if you hated the pool like I did, you were pretty much screwed.

But I needed to get my license. I'd thought up another plan on the drive this morning. Play the sympathy card. I figured if Mom saw how hard I was trying, how much I practiced, and how diligent I'd been, then maybe she'd see how bad a swimmer I was—naturally, through no fault of mine—and cut me a break.

She'd see I was giving it my Best Shot and forget about her stupid swim-to-drive deal. She was real big on giving things your Best Shot, and if I could convince her I was giving swimming my Best Shot, then maybe I stood a chance. As one of my Little League coaches always used to say when Andy Klatz struck out, "you can't get blood out of a turnip." When it came to swimming, I was as big a turnip as there was.

The family of five detoured to the kiddie pool, and I found a trio of chairs near the big pool. Of course, "big" was relative. This so-called resort pool was smaller than our neighborhood pool, and not any fancier. Just a rectangular hole filled with water. Not only that, but the chaise lounges were covered with some kind of tree pollen or something. There weren't problems like this at the beach.

I spread out my towel, making sure the yellowish-green tree gunk didn't get all over me, and unpacked Mom's tote bag. A romance novel, sunscreen, a book of crossword puzzles, an issue of *Guns and Ammo*—Jason's, no doubt—and a bag of trail mix. Livin' large, all right.

Keeping one eye on the entrance for Mom and Jason, I took in the scene. Lots of families, with lots of little kids running around. Hardly anyone my age on the concrete deck. The pool itself was crowded, but again, it was mostly kids with tons of toys. Noodles, inflatables, Frisbees, water bombs, supersoakers. It seemed anything was fair game. Things were a lot noisier here than at home, which brought a ray of hope. Maybe Mom wouldn't be able to stand all the commotion, and we could leave. Say goodbye to this bogus resort and go home. *All* the way home.

A few minutes later, Mom and Jason strode toward me, holding hands. When she saw me, she waved, and instead of waving back, I pulled the baseball cap lower on my head and pretended I was sleeping.

"Time for some sun," she said, claiming the chair farthest from me, while Jason flopped down on the one between us. "Did we miss anything?"

I pushed my cap up and grunted. "Nope. Nothing. Except you missed the guy parasailing. And another guy caught a twenty-foot marlin." I craned my head around, searching. "I guess they left, though."

Next to me, Jason suppressed a laugh, but Mom wasn't amused. I guess she'd become immune to my wit over the years. "Listen, Nick-o. This is our vacation. If you want to be a grumpus, feel free. Just don't wreck things for me and Jason, okay? Hand me my book, will ya?"

A grumpus? That was a new one. I gave her book to Jason, who relayed it to Mom. Then I passed him his magazine.

"Thanks." He flicked the cover with his finger, then flipped it open. "Gotta keep current."

I figured it was time to get wet and show Mom how hard I'd been working before she got too engrossed in her cheesy book. "I guess I'd better get swimming," I said in a voice louder than necessary.

Mom dipped her book down and peered at me over the top.

I rose from my chair. "Yeah, even though we're on vacation, I need to practice. Can't take a day off, you know. Too much at stake." I patted my gut and started waving my arms around, really hamming it up. Mom stared at me, not quite sure what to make of things. "I've been working very hard at this, and I hope it will pay off." I thought about adding some more, but I already felt I was pushing the envelope.

I walked over to the edge of the pool and took a deep breath. I was pretty sure Mom was watching, but I didn't want to glance over my shoulder. Better to jump in and look later. I took a deep breath and hopped in.

Even though I knew what was coming, even though I'd been through it dozens of times in the past month, the shock of the cold water rippled through me and stole my breath away. And every time it happened, my first thought was to haul my ass out of the pool and wrap myself in a towel and vow never to go in the water again.

Then I would see a vision of me in the future, on a date, getting driven places by Miller so I gritted my teeth and stayed in the pool.

To be fair, I always warmed up pretty quickly, but those initial seconds always put me in a crappy mood. Was it any wonder I hated swimming?

I dunked my head under to get my hair wet and glanced back at Mom and Jason when I surfaced. He'd gone back to his magazine—if he'd ever left it—but Mom had the book face down in her lap. Unfortunately,

117

her shades made it difficult to tell if she was looking in my direction, or if she was staring off into space, contemplating the meaning of our existence.

I began with a few warm-up exercises Allie gave me. Stretching arms and legs, in parts and in certain combinations. I was sure I looked like a goof, but I wasn't as self-conscious here as I was at home—I didn't know anybody, and I didn't much care what a bunch of ten-year-olds thought about me. Of course, they probably weren't even looking in my direction. Probably.

As I moved into some breathing exercises, a group of girls filed past on the pool deck. Four of them, they seemed to be about my age, and from my vantage point, they all seemed ... interesting.

So much for not being self-conscious. I rubbed some pretend water from my eyes and tracked them as they found a place to lie out. Down the row, about ten or twelve chairs from where we sat.

As they settled in, I glanced back at Mom and Jason. Mom had returned to her book, but Jason was ogling the new arrivals. He could give Miller a few lessons.

He turned in my direction, and we locked eyes. His expression changed as he realized I'd busted him checking out girls almost half his age. He gave a little shrug and an uneasy smile, then raised the magazine in front of his face.

I shot another look down at the girls. Three of them were busy stripping off clothes and putting on sunscreen and messing with sunglasses and hats and drinks. The fourth, a curvy redhead, was staring right at me with what I chose to believe was a slight smile.

With astonishing speed, I glanced away and waited for my adrenaline rush to subside. I sucked in a few deep breaths and returned to my swimming drills, but it was no use. I was toast. Now, every five seconds, I knew what I'd be thinking about—and it wasn't swimming. So much for not feeling self-conscious. And so much for learning to swim.

I spent the next few minutes mostly bobbing up and down. I didn't want to do any more drills, just in case someone—a hot sixteen-year-old girl, to be specific—was watching and recognized me for what I was: a loser who couldn't swim. And I didn't want to venture a direct glance in their direction, just in case one happened to be checking me out. Didn't want to seem too sex-starved or creepy or geeky or whatever. I wanted to be *cool*. So I bobbed up and down like a cool chunk of driftwood, straining to catch a glimpse of them in my peripheral vision.

I was about to give up my lame quest and drag myself from the water when I sensed a presence behind me. I spun around, ready to dodge some kid swinging a pool noodle. Instead, I came face-to-face with the redhead. Somehow, she'd outflanked my keen surveillance.

"Hi," she said, in the cutest voice I'd heard since we arrived at this stupid resort. Only a few hours, I know, but still...

"Hey." This cool driftwood's pulse had accelerated.

"My name's Emily." She pointed out of the pool in the direction of her friends. "We saw you in the pool, all alone, and thought we'd say hi. I got the short straw."

"Huh? The short straw?" I followed her finger toward her friends, who were all gawking at us. Like a car wreck?

"Just joking." The sun was in her eyes, forcing her to squint at me. "What's your name?"

"Nick. Nick Carlin."

"Pleased to meet you, Nick Carlin." She slicked back her red hair, and I noticed her cream-colored skin was perfectly smooth, like the ceramic vase Gram had on a table in her living room.

"It's nice to meet you, too, Emily."

"Where are you from?"

I told her where I lived, and she told me she lived near Frederick. In Maryland. "I've never been there," I said.

"Well, you're not missing much. We're here for the weekend, visiting my friend's uncle. He owns one of the condos on the other side of the *resort*." She put air-quotes around the word resort.

I laughed. "Yeah. Some *resort*." I put more exaggeration into my air quotes, and she laughed too.

"Could this place be any lamer?" she asked. "Well, at least they have a pool, right?"

"Uh, yeah," I said, giving the surface of the water a playful slap. "I love swimming pools."

Chapter Seventeen

I stood near the entrance to the Tree Tops Corral, waiting for Emily. We'd made plans to meet here for the resort's Saturday Night Chuckwagon Feast. Evidently, it was offered free to all the guests—all you had to do was show a room or cabin key. I hoped it wasn't a "you get what you pay for" deal.

The corral consisted of about thirty picnic tables set up in a giant circle. An old-fashioned split rail fence surrounded the whole clearing, but it seemed every third split rail was missing. On one side, behind some of the tables, four or five metal drums had been cut in half and filled with charcoal to serve as grills. Huge plumes of smoke rose into the evening sky, and lines of hungry resort-goers waited for their grub to be ready.

I was kinda surprised Mom and Jason had allowed me to come by myself—they said the afternoon of sun worshipping had taken the fight out of them. I figured it was just an excuse to get rid of me and have some alone time, but whatever. It was better for me, anyway.

The day had turned out to be pretty darn good. Emily and I had hung out the rest of the afternoon. She'd introduced me to her friends who seemed cool, then we found a couple chairs close to the guy running the poolside trivia contest. As big as a bear with a voice to match, he sported a huge, waxed handlebar moustache that looked so fake we kept waiting for it to fall into the glass of water he kept sipping from.

We were too busy cracking jokes and ragging on him to answer a single one of the questions correctly. He glared at us on more than a few occasions, but we couldn't help ourselves. I guess he wasn't used to trivia contest hecklers, although we kept the comments to ourselves. Mostly.

All afternoon while I was with Emily, I kept expecting a tap on the shoulder from Mom or Jason, telling me it was time to leave, but they didn't bother me. They must have figured that as long as I was occupied, they'd have some peace and quiet. Thank goodness for small favors.

A steady stream of people made their way into the corral. Like at the pool, it was mostly families. I was supposed to meet Emily here at eight o'clock, so I took out my phone to check the time. I waited a moment for it to find a signal. Service here had been spotty, and since I'd forgotten to pack my charger, I'd turned the phone off earlier in the day. After a moment, two bars showed up right along with the time: 8:08. Something else: six text messages waited.

I read the first one. Miller wanted to know if I'd been busted sneaking out. Figures. I moved on to the next one. It was from Laura. My heart skipped. What did she want? To gloat about hooking up with Air Force? Part of me wanted to delete it unread, but I opened it. She wanted to talk about what happened last night. I checked the time. She'd sent it at 10:30 this morning. What *did* happen last night? I pictured Laura and Air Force in the back of a van, his hands all over her.

I opened the next message. From Laura. And the next, and the next. All from Laura. All with variations on the first message. *I need to talk to you about last night.* If it had been Miller leaving so many messages, or even Johnny B, I'd think they *did* want to brag about it. But that wasn't Laura's style. She may have hooked up with a geek like Air Force, but she wasn't the type to rub my face in it.

Maybe she wanted to apologize.

Maybe she saw the error of her ways and wanted to give me another chance.

There was only one thing to do. Send a text message. To Miller.

My fingers danced on the keys: *Hear anything about AF and Laura?*

A few seconds later: *AF probably tapped it, brb*

I didn't have time to wait. *Cya.* I figured Miller was talking out of his ass again. If he knew something solid, he would have texted me earlier.

Only one way to know what was on Laura's mind. Go straight to the source. I started to compose a response to her in my head, but what could I text beyond, "Sure, let's talk"? Texting was great for most things, but this situation needed a phone call. There was so much more you could tell from someone's actual voice.

I was about to hit her number when I spotted Emily walking down the mulched path from the far side of the resort. She wore white shorts and a pale green shirt, and she carried a little purple purse over one shoulder. She'd done something different to her hair that made her look more exotic, and I knew if Jason were standing next to me, I'd get a poke in the ribs accompanied by a leer.

"Hey, Emily," I called, waving her over. I wasn't sure if she'd be bringing her friends along, but I wasn't disappointed to see she hadn't.

"Hi, Nick." She stopped and looked me up and down. "Where are the cowboy boots and ten-gallon hat? Ain't this a cookout, pardner?" She'd turned on a Texas cowboy accent and pretended to spit after she spoke.

"Sho nuff, ma'am," I said, tipping the brim of my imaginary hat. "I'm looking forward to some bar-be-qued armadillo. Hear they're mighty fine eatin'."

She play-slapped me on the arm, setting the fine hairs on my arms dancing. Suddenly, I was *very* glad Mom and Jason decided to stay in, although I'd be changing my tune if Jason really did pop the question tonight. "Hungry? I am. I could eat a barbequed horse."

"Sure, I'm starved. Let's go." I was kidding about the armadillos; I hoped she was kidding about the horse. I'd heard stories about West Virginia.

We got in line behind an older couple, both dressed in jeans and cowboy shirts. Had the rodeo come to town? We chatted about nothing in particular, and when she leaned in to say something especially witty, I caught a whiff of something. Alcoholic, with a vague fruity smell underneath.

Five minutes later, our plates were full of chuckwagon grub, although it seemed like I'd managed to get twice as much food as she had. A hamburger, a hot dog, chili, home fries, and a piece of corn on the cob that looked like it had been cooking since the Civil War. We found two seats on the end of a picnic table, far enough away from anyone else so we wouldn't have to talk to strangers.

"This cookout thing is kind of hokey, but I like it," Emily said, ripping open a little packet of mustard to put on her hot dog. "Last year I think I had three helpings of the home fries."

"You came last year?" I'd wolfed down my hot dog already and was about to start in on my hamburger. I'd tried the home fries and they were too greasy, which for me, was really saying something.

She took a bite of her hot dog, and a small yellow blob of mustard stuck to the side of her mouth. She licked it off with a sideways flick of the tongue. "Yeah. This is our third 'girls' weekend. My friend's uncle likes to show off his place, I guess."

"This is my first time."

"First time, eh?" She put on a wicked grin. "So, you're a Tree Tops virgin."

"Uh, yeah, I suppose."

She went back to her meal, and I focused on mine. The chili was especially spicy, and, unfortunately, the corn on the cob tasted like it looked. I put it down after one bite. Darkness had arrived suddenly, but a series of spotlights set up on poles surrounding the corral lent a festive air to the shindig. Out of the corner of my eye, I noticed someone coming toward us.

Jason.

His grin grew when he saw Emily. He carried two trays in his hands, both mounded high with food. I didn't see Mom; maybe she was getting their drinks.

Luckily, Emily and I were almost finished. In a few minutes, after some polite conversation with Mom and Jason, we could excuse ourselves and split, on to more promising things.

But Jason didn't take a seat. Instead, he loomed over us, balancing the trays, the tendons in his forearms bulging. "Hey there, Nick. How's dinner?" His grin seemed diabolical in the weird shadows created by the spotlights.

"Fine," I said.

Jason tilted his head toward Emily. "Who's your friend?"

I introduced them, and I couldn't help notice how Emily's face perked up in response to Jason's attention.

"Nice to meet you, Emily." Jason turned to me, and any trace of a smile had disappeared. "Could I talk to you for a moment?"

"Sure."

Jason cleared his throat.

Emily got up. "Oh, that's okay. I'll just go get some dessert. I think I saw those little ice cream cups. Want one?"

"Sounds good," I said.

She slid out from the bench, coming within inches of Jason, and flipped her head back, just touching him with a few strands of hair. "Be right back." Her words, her eyes, her movements all were directed at Jason.

I watched her walk away and noticed Jason's eyes tracking her, too.

When she was halfway across the corral, Jason took her seat.

"Where's Mom?"

"She's back at the cabin. I'm getting us a little take-out." He leaned in toward me. "Listen, champ. I'm all for sowing oats and having fun and all that, but you need to be careful. Your friend looks a little on the young side. Don't want to be looking at the wrong end of a shotgun, do you?"

Had Mom sent him to check up on me? "She's my age. She told me."

Jason nodded his head slowly. "Maybe she is. Maybe she isn't. What I'm saying is you have to be real careful. She doesn't look...Girls will..." Now his head shook, from side to side. "Just be careful. For your own sake. Remember: there are plenty of fish in the lagoon. Keep your harpoon in your pants, for now. That's my best advice."

I'd had enough of Jason's friendly advice. "I've got this under control. So, if you'll excuse me, I'm going to find Emily." I rose and grabbed Emily's tray, balancing it on top of mine. "Don't wait up."

"Be home by midnight," Jason called out to my back as I stomped off toward the trash can.

I found Emily in line at the dessert station. When it was our turn, we each took a vanilla ice cream cup and a flat wooden spoon to eat it with. Old school, as Gram would say. We found a level dry spot on the ground just outside the corral and ate our ice cream in silence. Well, it was mostly silent, except for a few questions Emily asked about Jason, which I answered with one-word grunts.

After we ate, she extracted a pack of cigarettes from her tiny purse. "Mind?"

I hated cigarettes—the smell, the smoke, the being addicted part. Mom had threatened to cut off my fingers if she ever caught me smoking a "cancer stick." Emily hadn't mentioned she smoked. "Go ahead."

"Want one?"

"Uh, no thanks."

She took her time lighting up, and I felt as if I were witnessing some sort of ritual. Banging the box on her knee a few times, carefully tapping out a cigarette. Flicking her lighter. Then she took a deep drag, turned her head, and tipped it skyward as she blew out a thin stream of smoke. "Nice. Smooth."

I scooted back a hair.

She eyed me as she took another puff. "Dinner was good, huh?"

"Yeah." In this light, and with the way she held her cigarette carefully in two fingers, she looked like a little girl playing grown-up. Had Jason been on to something?

"So, what year were you born?" I asked, as casually as I could.

"Huh?" She hesitated, and I could almost see the gears turning behind her green eyes. "Why, the same year as you were, silly." She giggled and took another puff, waving her hand to dissipate the smoke. "So, what do you feel like doing now?"

"I don't know. Why don't we—"

"Let's go for a walk. I know this great place." Without waiting for an answer, she grabbed my hand, pulled me up from the ground, and tugged me along. She led me down the path away from the corral and lodge, at a good clip, humming some song I couldn't quite place. After a final puff, she flicked her cigarette butt into some bushes.

The lights from the corral gradually faded, but the moon was nearly full, and it cast an eerie glow. When we came to a fork in the trail, we peeled off to the right, following an old wooden sign that read simply "Lake."

After a while, the path opened up, and I was able to pull alongside her. She let go of my hand and slowed, searching the left side of the trail for something. "I know it's here somewhere."

"What is?" I asked, half afraid it was the carcass of some woodland creature she thought would be cool to gross me out with. I suddenly realized I didn't know Emily all that well. Jason's words echoed in my head. *Just be careful.* "What are we looking for?"

"Over here," she said, pointing into a thicket.

I hustled over and found her standing next to a narrow foot-trail through the brush.

"Come on," she said, as she dug her phone out of her purse. She held it over her head like the Statue of Liberty, a beacon to follow. "This way." She disappeared into the woods.

I followed.

We seemed to be going down a slight incline, and, in spots, the path narrowed to almost a wisp, but we were able to pick it up again each time. Emily kept humming as we plunged on.

"Where are we going?"

She stopped and spun around, bringing the phone down from over her head. "You'll see when we get there. Which should be very soon." She resumed her little song as we kept going.

The bugs were nipping at my exposed skin, and I was afraid I was going to walk into a sharp branch, but I didn't want to stop, afraid Emily would think I was a wimp. I couldn't help wondering if people really liked hiking, or if they just liked wearing hiking boots and shopping at REI.

"Here we go." Emily's phone went dark, and the trees fell away, and we were at a little sandy beach area on the edge of the lake. Overhead, the moon reflected off the surface of the water. Pretty cool. And pretty isolated. "I'm going for a swim," she said. "Coming?"

She yanked off her shirt and tossed it aside. She was facing away from me, but she had a terrific back. I stood there frozen, watching. Keeping her back to me and humming the same song, she unbuttoned her shorts. Then she wriggled out of them, giving me a pretty good look at her in bra and panties.

She looked mighty fine in the moonlight.

My heart leaped into my throat.

She still hadn't glanced at me. With a whoop, she ran into the water, splashing and kicking up spray. She kept going until she had to tread water. The whole time, when I probably should have been taking off my own clothes, I stood there like a statue of Peeping Tom.

It didn't take long for Emily to realize I was still on terra firma. "Hey, come on. What's the problem?"

I tried to come up with some reason why I couldn't join her but telling her I couldn't swim didn't seem to be the way to go.

"The water's great. Come on." As she treaded water, all I could see was her head, but the image of her almost naked body had been seared into my retinas for life. "I'm lonely out here."

"How deep is it?" I called back.

"Plenty deep. Why, do you want to do some diving?" The amusement in her tone was unmistakable.

"I don't know."

"I thought you loved the pool. Think of this as a large pool," she said. "By the way, I'm not wearing many clothes."

Just because I couldn't swim didn't mean I was blind. "I noticed."

"I was hoping you would." She laughed. "Come on. The water's nice and cool!"

I looked up at the moon, and it looked back. I was sure the Man in the Moon was mocking me for my cowardice.

Fuck that.

There were certain times in a person's life where you just had to leave your fears behind and go for it.

I peeled off my shirt and practically jumped out of my pants, glad that I'd decided to wear one of my newer pairs of boxers.

I dashed toward the water, determined to dive right in. When my feet hit the cold water, I fought the urge to turn around. I sloshed into the lake, going until it reached my neck, gasping for breath as the cold water seemed to squeeze the air from my lungs.

My strategy was simple. Use what I'd learned during my swim lessons. Allie said I was ready, that I just needed to put it all together. Now was my chance. Stroke, kick, breathe. Stroke, kick, breathe. Three things. Simple. I could do it. A surge of confidence roared through my body.

Once I reached Emily, she could help me stay afloat, if need be.

"I'm waiting," Emily yelled.

I took a few more steps and felt the bottom of the lake disappear. I took a big gulp of air, then began swimming. I took a couple of strokes toward her, but it was pretty dark, and I had trouble telling exactly where she was.

I heard her calling out, so I shifted direction. Took a few more strokes, then blew some bubbles out, then I forgot to kick while I turned my head to breathe. My hips sank, my face went under, but I tried to breathe anyway and got a mouthful of water. I flung my head up out of the water and sucked in a giant lungful of air. I heard Emily in the background calling to me, but I couldn't tell if she was three feet away or thirty.

I began to sink in the water, and my muscles stopped working. In my mind's eye, I saw Uncle Steve grab his chest and flop into the water. I saw myself, curled up on the bottom of the boat, crying.

I saw the divers haul his dead body out of the water. I saw Aunt Barrie and my mom hugging each other, wailing.

My head bobbed up, then down, then up, and then I went completely under. I thrashed about, pawing at the water, splashing and kicking, but the more I struggled, the deeper I seemed to sink. I tried to turn around and head for shore, but I was so disoriented I didn't know which way that was—I couldn't even tell which way was up anymore. I knew—just knew—that I'd never feel fresh air on my face again.

I pictured my mother, bending over my casket at the funeral, her tears dripping on my corpse.

I windmilled my arms faster, trying to power myself up to the surface. I kicked like I'd never kicked before. With every passing second, my lungs cried out in despair.

Fueled by a final burst of adrenaline, I marshalled every ounce of energy—or was it panic?—that I possessed, and with a frantic series of strokes, I somehow managed to surface.

I sucked in a huge breath. "Help!" I sputtered. "Help!"

I slapped the water furiously, trying to stay afloat. Ten seconds later, Emily's arm circled my neck. "Relax, Nick. I'll help you."

"Thanks," I managed to spit out, along with a mouthful of water.

Keeping my head above water, she towed me in, like the derelict vessel I was.

"You can stand now," she said as we approached shore.

I put my feet down, and she let go of me.

"Uh, thanks," I said, still gulping air.

"Yeah. No problem."

We walked ashore, and I fell to my knees, still gasping. Still trembling, too, from the fear. And maybe more so from the embarrassment.

Emily went straight for her clothes. Put them on without a word. Then she looked at me, disappointment in her eyes.

Yeah, I knew that look.

"I think I want to go back now, okay?" she said.

We trudged back to civilization in utter silence.

We didn't exchange numbers.

Chapter Eighteen: T-minus 5 days

Gulp

Miller and I were playing H-O-R-S-E at one of the Pettigrew Park basketball courts. Was it only last Wednesday when Laura had asked me to the party? It seemed like it had been five months ago.

Miller dribbled the ball behind his back, then did a 180-degree turn in mid-air and heaved the ball at the basket. It caromed off the backboard, then clanged off the rim. No good. Miller sucked at basketball, but he sometimes beat me in H-O-R-S-E because he spent hours working up these circus shots. "Dang. I've been practicing that one."

"You need more practice." I grabbed the ball.

"Where's Johnny B this week?" Miller leaned against the pole, waiting for me to take my turn.

"Young Leaders conference, I think." I took a few dribbles, trying to decide which shot to choose from my arsenal. I needed to find one I could sink, but he couldn't.

"He went to that one a few weeks ago. This week he must be at computer camp." Miller scoffed. "Man, his parents must hate him. Shipping him out all summer."

I eyed the basket, visualizing a left-handed hook shot. If I made it, I'd give Miller a letter; he couldn't hit his face with his left hand. "Maybe his parents love him and want him to pursue his interests."

"Or maybe his parents want to get rid of him so they can enjoy their lives."

I decided I'd save my left-handed shot for the coup de grace. I dribbled to the foul line. "Okay, ready?"

"Let 'er rip."

I turned around so my back was to the basket and set my heels up against the white line. After a peek at the hoop over my shoulder, I heaved it over my head without looking. It soared about five feet over the backboard and started bouncing toward the baseball field. I could make up wild shots, too.

"Man, we both suck." Miller jogged off to retrieve the ball. When he returned, instead of taking his turn, he sat on it, and his face drooped, and I didn't think it was from the heat.

I sat on the blacktop across from him. "What's wrong?"

"Everything. This morning my dad got on my case again. Started talking seriously about sending me off to military school. Military *boarding* school. My parents want to ship me out."

"Hey, maybe you could wind up like Air Force. Flying jets somewhere in the wild blue yonder." I pictured Air Force with his arm around Laura, and my stomach lurched. I took a deep breath and fought hard to banish the image. I'd tried texting—and calling—her since I got back from our so-called vacation, but she hadn't responded. And I'd been too chicken to show up at her house in person, afraid that maybe I *would* bump into him there.

Miller scowled. "This is serious. They're serious. They want to retire, and I'm their last obstacle. Sometimes I think I'm going to go home, and they'll have moved out. No forwarding address."

"Come on, your parents wouldn't do that." Miller's grades sucked, and his behavior was often worse. Still, military school was harsh.

133

"Bullshit they wouldn't. You should have seen the evil gleam in my dad's eyes. He's still pissed about what I did to Kelly."

I didn't know the details of Miller's latest transgression, but I was pretty sure he deserved his father's ire. He had a severe problem with authority. "He'll cool down. He always does."

That seemed to calm Miller. "Maybe. If he doesn't, I'm going to kill myself. I don't think military boarding school is the right place for me, dude." He sighed. "Enough of my stupid problems. Let's move on to yours. Did your step-dad-to-be pop the question to your mom?"

I shrugged. "I don't know. You trying to make me ill?"

"What do you mean you don't know? How can you not know?"

"Mom didn't say anything. How am I supposed to know?" On the next court over, a three-on-three game was getting started. They were going to shoot for teams and were arguing about who would shoot first.

"You would know. Your mom would be flashing her ring around, holding her hand in your face, admiring how the ring glinted in the light. There'd be a lot of oohing and aahhing. Don't you watch any movies?"

I watched plenty of movies, and Miller knew it, because we watched most of them together. "Life isn't some romantic movie where everyone lives happily ever after, you know."

"Believe me, I know. Mine's turning into a horror flick." He still sat on the basketball, and now he rolled back and forth on it. "You getting along with this guy any better?"

"I don't know. Sometimes he seems all right. He let me sneak out to the party. But..." I held my hands out, palms up.

"What?"

"Sometimes I get a bad vibe from him."

"A bad vibe? What are you, a medium?" Miller snorted.

"You know, a bad feeling. He seems kinda slimy, kinda sketchy. Like there's a whole lot of secrets underneath. Secrets that if we found out, we wouldn't like. Know what I mean?"

"You're full of it sometimes. He didn't rat you out, and he likes your mom—who's pretty hot, by the way. I don't know if I've mentioned it lately."

I glared at him, like I always did when he went on about my mom.

"Look, if it's bothering you so much, do a little snooping." Miller arched an eyebrow.

"What are you talking about?"

"Scavenger hunt. Search for buried treasure. Toss the joint. Shake out the place."

I stared at him, waiting for him to get to his point in a way I could understand.

"Dude, look for the ring."

"You want me to search through his stuff looking for my mother's engagement ring?"

"Hey, why not? You don't *for sure* know it's an engagement ring. It could be a charm bracelet or something. Maybe it's a hundred-dollar bill, all folded up. My uncle did that to my aunt once. I don't think she liked that surprise, come to think of it."

I shook my head. Miller definitely had a few screws loose.

"What? It'll put your mind at ease, one way or the other. You'll either know you're getting a step-dad, or you'll be relieved you're not." He shrugged. "At least not yet."

"Seems a bit desperate. Or paranoid. Or something."

"Come on. Are you telling me you've never snooped around in your mother's stuff?" Miller asked, eyes bright.

"Yeah. That's what I'm saying. I'm not a perv like you."

Miller shrugged. "I'm not a perv. I'm just curious. I go through my sisters' stuff all the time. You never know what you might find. You should consider it a fact-finding mission. Why, it's practically your

135

duty to know what's going on in your own home."

"And if I find the ring? I'm just supposed to pretend like nothing's going to happen?" I shook my head. I didn't know if I was that good an actor.

"Don't worry. Your mom and her boyfriend probably aren't paying that much attention to you. They've only got eyes for each other." Miller batted his eyelashes, puckered his lips, and made smooching noises.

I sighed. "Whatever. Ring or no ring, there's not much I can do about it, is there?"

"You got that right. Let's talk about something you have control over. Your thing with Laura."

"What are you—"

Miller talked right over me. "Despite your vocal protests, Johnny B and I know who you're hot for. And your text the other night proved it. You can't stop thinking about Laura. You want her." He paused, dipping his head slightly as he closed his eyes for a moment. "It's okay. You have our blessing."

"Well, with your blessing, my life is fulfilled. I can die a happy man."

Miller rolled his eyes. "You can't let Air Force move in."

Seems like he already had. You snooze, you lose. "I don't know. I think I blew my chance with her. She was pretty hurt when I said I couldn't go to the party with her, and then I showed up. It was like I totally dissed her."

"Air Force is a dweeb. Given the choice between you and him, Laura would probably pick you. *Probably.*"

"Thanks a lot."

"Seriously, he's a goof. All you have to do is ask her out, be cool, say funny stuff, and you're golden. You need to put up a fight for her." Miller drummed a *bum-de-bum-bump* on the basketball. "Can I be the best man at the wedding?"

"Screw you."

"You're awful sensitive. You know what that means. I've hit a sore spot." He started laughing, and the snicker grew into a gale.

"I'll give *you* a sore spot." I made a fist.

Miller's laughter tapered off. "Like I said, awful sensitive."

I got up and brushed off a few pebbles stuck to my shorts. "I've got something I need to do. Check you later."

Miller looked hurt, as if I were abandoning him. "Uh, sure. See you later." He got up and held the ball on one hip like a short, pudgy Kobe Bryant. "Where are you going?"

"Believe it or not, I'm going to follow your advice. Adios." I hopped on my bike and started pedaling away. When I glanced over my shoulder, Miller was still staring at me, ball on hip.

* * *

I found Laura around the back of her house, on the deck, with her head stuck in a book. If any of my other friends had been reading a book, I would have been worried. But Laura definitely seemed like a girl who enjoyed a good read now and then.

"Hey."

She looked up, and her expression of surprise morphed into a smile, a bright one. "Hey, yourself." She slipped a bookmark into her book and set it on the table at her elbow, next to a can of root beer.

"I hope it's all right I dropped by. You weren't answering my texts, and I was…"

She arched one eyebrow. "What? Worried?"

I half-shrugged, half-nodded.

"Pull up a seat." Her smile returned.

I dragged a chair over and sat. "It's nice back here."

"Yeah, quiet." The deck overlooked a thick stretch of woods. From

137

where we sat, you couldn't see a sign of any neighboring houses. Only the faint hum of cars going by on a nearby street reminded you there were other people around. "Want a soda?"

"Sure. What you're drinking is good."

"Okay. Be right back." She got up and went inside, and I got a good look at her outfit. Nice-fitting shorts over tan, trim legs. A t-shirt adorned with palm trees. It fit nicely, too.

She returned a minute later and handed me a can of root beer. I popped it open and held it up. "Cheers."

She picked hers up and tapped it against mine. "Cheers to you." Then she took a gulp.

I did the same, trying to grease my suddenly dry mouth. On the bike ride over, I'd screwed up my courage to ask her out, but I realized it most likely would change our relationship from friends into something else. Better or worse. Which way it went depended on her answer, I guess. "Listen, I—"

"Wait. There's something I need to say. I'm sorry I made things weird between us by asking you to the party the other night. I should never have done that—in fact, I was mad at myself for doing it." The words spilled out quickly, as if she'd rehearsed the lines before delivering them.

"Don't be mad, it's—"

"Please, let me finish." She forced a smile. "I would never do anything to jeopardize our friendship. It means too much to me. I don't know what I was thinking, I just…"

I wanted to reach over and hold her hand, to calm her down, but I just sat still, afraid I would be the one to make things weird. Weirder than they already were, anyway. "It's okay. Really."

"Well, I'm sorry. I should have realized that if you wanted to go to the party, you'd want to go alone, or with the guys. Going with me would have just made things awkward for you." Her pace had slowed, and I wasn't sure if she was still working from her script, or if she had begun ad-libbing.

Either way, she had it all wrong. I'd gone to the party to talk to *her*, not cruise for other girls. I bit my lip as I decided whether to tell her that. Talk about making things weird!

"By the way, you didn't have to lie about going away for the weekend—I mean, I was still going to the party, even without you." Her features tensed.

"It wasn't a lie. We did go away. It's just we didn't leave until Saturday morning." No need to get into the details.

She cocked her head, and I got the feeling she was deciding whether to believe me or not. Then she brightened. "I guess it turned out okay, huh? You went to the party anyway, and I got to know Harmon. I know you guys don't like him much, but he's pretty cool underneath the surface. I have a feeling I'm going to be seeing him a lot, and I really—really—hope you'll try to get along with him. It's important to me."

"Uh, sure." My stomach soured, and I made a mental note to keep any Air Force wisecracks to myself. I'd come over here to ask Laura out; now that seemed like an exercise in futility. I'd get shot down in a second. I took a long swig of root beer as I tried to think of something to say—something to let her know I wanted to go out with her, without actually telling her I wanted to go out with her. My mind was in too much of a pretzel to come up with anything remotely plausible. I ran a finger around the rim of my can of soda and waited for Laura to say something. Anything.

A moment passed between us, and it was like we each had something we wanted to get off our chest but were afraid to. Then it passed right along with a cool breeze that blew some hair into Laura's face. She pushed it aside. "The swimming going any better?"

I hadn't made any progress during this morning's lesson, in fact, I think I regressed some. "Not really. I just don't think this body was made for the water."

"I still don't think it's a problem with the body." She tapped her head, just like she did at the pond the other day. "Did you think any more about any possible psychological hang-ups?"

I had given it some thought but hadn't come up with anything. Of course, I'd been thinking of why I couldn't swim for ten years without coming to any conclusions. "I have no idea what my problem is."

She shrugged. "Maybe you need a new swim instructor. I could help you out. I was on the swim team for, like, six years."

"I don't think it's the fault of the instructor. Allie Merskie's teaching me now, ever since Dante got fired," I said.

"Oh." Laura said. "Allie Merskie. I bet she's good." She glanced at a bird swooping by, then her gaze settled on the can of root beer in her hand.

"Uh, yeah. She seems to know what she's doing."

"I'm sure she does." She waved at a wasp buzzing around her soda. It flew off, and she returned her attention to me. "You going to make it? Pass the test so you can get your license?"

"I better. The thought of not being able to drive for two years isn't pleasant. I mean, I'll have to get Miller to haul me around. In case you hadn't noticed, he can be kind of a jerk at times."

"I noticed."

"I figured." I took a sip of root beer.

"I'd give you a ride, if you needed a lift," she said, then realizing how her words might have been taken, her cheeks colored, and she glanced away.

I opened my mouth to continue the double-entendre thread but closed it without saying anything. Two weeks ago, we would have had a field day, laughing and trading barbs, seeing how far we could stretch the thread without breaking it. Now, things were awkward, no matter how much we tried to pretend otherwise. And we both seemed to know it.

I rose. "Well, I guess I need to get going. Thanks for the root beer."

"Anytime, Nick. Thanks for stopping by. I guess I'll see you around."

"Yeah, sure." I left, knowing I'd see her around, all right, but it would be in the arms of another guy.

Chapter Nineteen

That night, we had Gram over for dinner. Before the meal started, Mom wanted to make a little announcement. My breath caught. The last time Mom made a *little announcement,* Jason had moved in. A terrible premonition slugged me in the gut as I pictured my mother in a wedding dress.

"Come now, everyone into the family room." Mom shepherded us like wayward sheep.

Gram mumbled something about a command performance as we took our seats. I shared the couch with Gram, and Jason, who had just come in from heating up the grill, plopped down in the recliner. Mom stood nervously in the middle of the room, waiting for us to get settled, like a first-grade teacher bringing her class in from recess. She massaged her temples with her hands.

I checked those hands very carefully. No ring visible. Maybe this announcement wouldn't be so bad after all.

What could be making Mom so nervous? It must have something to do with Gram being there. This was the first time Gram and Jason would be spending some time together, aside from the one brunch at Gram's. And I wasn't sure that counted, because Gram had seemed a bit buzzed on mimosas. Tonight, she appeared to be completely sober and in full cantankerous-Gram mode, the way she got when Mom forced her to do something she didn't want to do.

"I'm thirsty. What have you got to drink?" Gram said, as if she'd been reading my mind and figured the only way to survive the evening was to get a little tipsy.

"Can you wait a minute?" Mom asked. It came out pretty snappish.

Gram eyed her. "I'm parched, dear." She made a noise halfway between a cough and a gag.

"Oh, for Pete's..." Mom sighed. "I made some lemonade. Nick, give me a hand, will you?" I followed her into the kitchen. She rolled her eyes at me as she grabbed a pitcher from the fridge. "Can you get some glasses?"

We returned to the family room, and Mom poured four glasses of lemonade. I handed one to Gram. "You made this? From actual lemons?" she asked. Although the question was directed at Mom, her gaze was firmly fixed on Jason.

"Well, from a mix. You know, that powder stuff. But it's just as good," Mom said.

Gram took a sip, then made a face as if she'd just found a skunk nesting in her skirt. "Oh, right. Just as good."

Mom forced a smile onto her face. "Would you like some water?"

"Oh, no. Don't go to any trouble. I'm fine." Gram repeated her cough-gag noise, although a little quieter this time.

I glanced at Jason. He looked calm and unruffled. Maybe he'd been sipping mimosas while he was firing up the grill. He caught me checking him out and winked. What was going on?

Mom wrung her hands. I hadn't seen her this nervous in...well, I couldn't remember ever seeing her like this. I knew how she felt—I'd been plenty nervous this afternoon before Laura squished my hopes as if she was stepping on a beetle. "First, let me thank you all for, um, coming tonight."

The "all" Mom was referring to must have been Gram. Jason and I pretty much always showed up for dinner—we lived there. Gram knew how nervous Mom was. And she slowly slid her bony elbow into my side to let me know she knew it.

Mom continued. "I have an announcement to make." Her eyes flitted from Jason to me to Gram, where they settled. "Jason and I are living together." After she said it, her whole body seemed to unwind, and the tension in her face vanished. She was good ol' Mom again.

"That's it?" Gram asked. "That's the big announcement?"

Mom looked puzzled, or maybe a little hurt. "I just wanted you to hear it from me that we're living together."

"For Chrissakes, child, I'm old, not stupid. I've known you two were shacking up since the day he moved in." She crooked her thumb at Jason, who sat serenely in the recliner with a vague smile on his face. Maybe he had a looney-tunes grandmother himself and knew what to expect. Gram wiped her brow with the back of her hand, hamming it up. "Frankly, I'm relieved."

"What do you mean?" Mom asked.

"I thought you were going to announce you were engaged." A small smile tugged at her wrinkled lips. "I'm relieved you're just living together."

I braced, waiting for Jason to explode. In my book—in many books—he'd just been dissed. But he just sat there with that stupid happy puppy-dog expression on his face. Had he somehow learned to go to sleep with his eyes wide open?

A mini-explosion did come, but it came from Mom. "How could you say something like that? What would be so wrong with getting married anyway?"

Gram turned her head toward Jason and squinted, like she was Dirty Harry from those old movies. Then she said, "Oh, nothing, I guess. But I suppose it would depend on who you were getting married *to*." She didn't take her eyes off Jason. Her squint intensified until you almost couldn't see any whites in her eyes. For a second, she reminded me of the Pool Czar.

Mom's jaw dropped. She took a step toward Jason, who hadn't moved, then stopped and rushed over to the couch. She grabbed Gram's hands and practically lifted her off the sofa. "Come with me, we need to have a talk. In private."

As Gram was being led from the room, she glanced over her shoulder at me and shrugged. I swear I detected a little mischievous smile on her face.

When they were gone, Jason let out a little chuckle. "Old ladies—no disrespect intended, of course—always crack me up. They think they can say anything they want, don't they? And they say some pretty funny stuff sometimes. Man, what I would give to be able to spout off like that without getting in trouble." He seemed amused, not pissed off in the least. He *must* have had his own version of Gram somewhere in his family. "So what's new with you?"

"Nothing much." I was a lot more discreet than Mom and Gram. My problems got discussed with my friends, not with my mother, and certainly not with my mother's boyfriend.

"I trust everything worked out okay with that girl at the resort."

"Don't worry, nothing happened."

"Wasn't worried. Glad you were careful, though. I can tell you're down about something else." His lip curled up on one side.

Was I that transparent? "No, I'm okay."

"It's the girl from the party, isn't it?" he asked. My surprise must have been evident, because he smiled like he'd just answered Final Jeopardy correctly with all his money on the line. "Don't worry, kid. I was your age once. I remember how it was. Feel like talking it over?"

"Thanks, but there's really not much to say. She's moved on." *Without me*, I felt like adding, but I guess that was obvious.

Jason sighed, and I knew what was coming. The lame more-fish-in-the-sea speech he was fond of giving. Maybe it was the only piece of advice he knew. "Nick. Forget her. There are plenty of barracudas—"

Mom and Gram entered the family room, and Jason leaned back in the recliner and pasted that ridiculous look of tranquility onto his face again.

Maybe I should take his advice and move on. Go fishing for another girl.

And I knew just the girl I was going to go after.

The Great White Whale.

Allie Merskie.

* * *

Allie Merskie knocked at my door at 10:56 on Tuesday morning with her brother Colin in tow. A math book was tucked under one of his arms, and a black-and-white composition book under the other. He didn't look happy to be on my doorstep.

"Come on in." I swung the door open. Allie wore some very short baby-blue shorts and a tank top. I didn't notice what Colin was wearing.

She stepped in. Colin remained on the porch until Allie turned around and motioned him in with an impatient wave of her arm. "Thanks for tutoring Colin here today." She lowered her voice, even though Colin was now standing right next to her. "My mom thought a change in scenery might help some." She whispered even more quietly. "Plus, he won't wander off here."

Colin rolled his eyes.

"Why don't you go into the kitchen, and I'll be there in a minute?" I pointed down the hall. Now was my chance to ask Allie out, and the last thing I needed was her brother listening in.

Colin shuffled down the hallway, muttering obscenities. Today's session was going to be another treat. He rounded the corner, and I turned my attention back to Allie, trying to ignore the twin rivers of sweat dripping down my armpits.

"I'm glad this tutoring thing is working out," she said. "I know my parents are really grateful for what you're doing."

I'd only met with Colin twice, and things were pretty rocky. And that was being kind. I guessed some adults believed what they wanted to believe. "Sure. Glad to help."

She smiled wider, and I had the urge to fetch my sunglasses so I wouldn't go blind. I took a deep breath and reviewed my strategy. First, some small talk to get her warmed up, then move in to seal the deal. "So, working at the pool today?"

"Yeah, I'm on in an hour. You going to come by to practice? Not much time before the test."

Three days, twenty-two hours. But who's counting? "Maybe. I know I should..." Yesterday's lesson went okay, but I still wasn't there yet. I think I needed more than a few more weeks of practice. Maybe a decade's worth.

"Nick. I've taught a lot of kids how to swim. You have all the physical tools, and we've gone over all the fundamentals—the strokes, kicking, breathing. Everything. I think it boils down to your attitude. You've got to believe in yourself. Work on the power of positive thinking," Allie sounded a lot like Laura. Was feeling negative something on the Y chromosome?

"Yeah, yeah. You're right." I held up my hand as if I were taking an oath. "I swear I will be more positive. I swear, I think I can swim. I swear I'll drown if I try to swim the length of the pool."

She pointed her finger at me. "No drowning allowed." Then she smiled again. "At least not on my watch."

She seemed warmed up enough. "Listen, Allie, I was sorta wondering if—"

A loud clanging noise from the basement interrupted me. It was followed by Colin's shouting. "Oh shit. OH, HOLY SHIT."

I raced down the hall and flew down the basement stairs, with Allie on my heels. We found Colin standing in the middle of Mom's menagerie with a gigantic, evil grin on his face. Six or seven of the cages had been opened, and the one that housed crickets was on the floor, top off. Crickets were everywhere, along with ants and beetles and mice. I darted over to the snake cages. Luckily, they hadn't been disturbed. I had the feeling that was only because Colin hadn't seen them yet.

"Colin Merskie, what did you do?" Allie said, using her "don't run on the pool deck" voice.

He shrugged. "I was just looking at the bugs and…"

Allie pressed her lips together, and I thought she might explode.

The thought of all these critters crawling around my house didn't thrill me, but the thought of what Mom might do had me petrified. A cricket hopped up and grazed my shin. "Don't worry about it," I said, trying to act like I meant it. "We can catch them all. I'm practically a professional. Let's try to get the mice first."

"Cool," Colin said.

I managed to corner a few of the mice and grab their tails. Back into the cage they went. The others had already taken refuge in whatever cracks or hidden recesses they could find. I'd worry about them later when they came out for food.

On to the bugs.

To her credit, Allie jumped right in, not afraid or squeamish in the least. We righted the cages, then armed ourselves with some shoeboxes. With the box in one hand and the top in the other, we tried to scoop up as many bugs as we could. I assigned Colin to try to round up the ants and beetles; they were slower and more predictable than the crazy crickets. But when it got right down to it, we all went after anything that crawled, hopped, or slithered, and we didn't worry about sorting them into their respective cages.

Any captured insect went into the closest cage. Then they were on their own. Survival of the fittest, and all that. Or more specifically, survival of the ones with the largest mouths.

The entire time we were hunting down the bugs, I tried to figure out a way to casually ask Allie out, but I knew I'd lost any chance of her being receptive now. No one wants to think about going on a date after picking up bugs for the better part of an hour. Not even easy-going Allie.

We did the best we could, then Allie left, and I tutored Colin. This time, he seemed a bit more cooperative and not as rambunctious. I guess liberating a thousand bugs had a calming effect on him.

* * *

After Colin left, I went back down to the basement. Everything seemed to have returned to normal, save for a few bugs I spotted crawling around in the corners. I didn't have the energy left to chase them down, so I turned off the lights and went upstairs.

The house was empty. Mom was working, and Jason was off somewhere—he didn't leave his whereabouts with me. I supposed he could have been on a job interview, but if I had to guess, I'd say it was more likely he was hiding in the woods somewhere dressed in camo clothes, waiting to shoot some poor defenseless animal.

What did Mom see in him, anyhow?

I grabbed a Sprite from the fridge and popped it open. Took it out onto the front porch and sat on the first step. I took a sip and watched a phalanx of ants march up the side of the concrete step toward a nearby boxwood bush. A couple of them had pieces of leaves in their tiny pincers. Amazing how such little creatures could carry such heavy stuff—at least relative to their size. I imagined what I'd look like carrying a Buick around over my head with one hand, following Johnny B and Miller, each toting their own vehicle. In my little daydream, Miller turned to me and asked me if I'd searched the house yet.

No, not yet.

Well, what are you waiting for?

Good question.

I rose, Sprite in hand, and dusted off my shorts. Shot a glance at the driveway to make sure Jason's car hadn't somehow gotten past me. Then I went inside to begin my fact-finding mission.

I sprang up the stairs and headed for my mom's bedroom. Never neat, it was even messier now that another occupant had moved in. I started on the far side of the room, where it looked like Jason had set up camp. A few bulging duffel bags rested on the floor, unopened. Some of his stuff was strewn across the top of a low dresser I'd helped move up from the basement last week. A mountain of dirty clothes rose up in the corner.

I set my Sprite on the top of the dresser and reached to open the uppermost drawer. Froze, just as my fingers touched the pull. What was I doing? Invading someone's privacy, just because I wanted to know what was going to happen to my life? Was it my *duty* as Miller claimed? Or was I simply being a jerk?

I thought of Jason's smarmy smile as he put his arm around Mom, and I pulled the drawer open. I'd do anything to protect my mother.

Underwear and socks. With a single finger, I gently pushed aside the clothes to see if anything was hiding in the back of the drawer. Nope, just more socks and underwear. I moved on to the next drawer. T-shirts, shorts. The bottom two drawers contained clothes, too, including at least three camo outfits. But I didn't find any engagement ring.

Next stop was the nightstand. I opened the single drawer. A box of condoms stared back at me. And not just any box of condoms—a

150

jumbo-sized economy box. My stomach did somersaults. I slammed the drawer closed and shut my eyes, trying to get the gymnast in my gut to sit still.

I dropped to my knees and peered under the bed. An army of dust bunnies had amassed, but aside from a few pencils and an old sock, nothing hid there.

I bounced back to my feet and took a break from my snooping to glance out the window. It was only about three o'clock, so I figured Mom would still be at work for a while—unless she got a cancellation or something. You never knew for sure. But I was more worried about Jason. What if he found me in his underwear drawer up to my elbows? He'd think I was a pervert, for sure. Or a thief. Neither was a good option.

The coast was still clear.

I took a deep breath and paused a moment to think things through. If I were Jason, where would I hide an engagement ring so my mom wouldn't find it? His car? I didn't think so. When they went out together, he always drove. Someplace in the garage? Probably not, Mom stored a lot of her pest control supplies out there and was always rooting around, searching for something she needed. Elsewhere in the house? No, he wouldn't know which place Mom might decide to clean next. Buried in an old beer can somewhere in the back yard? Although that sounded more like Jason's style, I doubted it.

The ring had to be hidden in his stuff, somewhere in the bedroom.

That left two choices: the duffel bags or the closet. I crossed the room to the small closet. Mom had a larger, walk-in closet where she kept most of her clothes. Before Jason had moved in, she used the smaller one for storing stuff we didn't use much, like tablecloths, old flannel sheets, and ski pants. At the same time, we hauled the dresser up from the basement; we'd transferred all the stuff from that closet down to the basement.

Jason had it about half-full. A bunch of dress shirts—gathering dust, mostly—and some pants on hangars. A few more camouflage garments. Shoes and boots. Some tote bags covered a large tackle box on the floor in the back.

I trotted over to the window again, just to make sure I didn't get caught. No sign of anyone, so I hustled back to the closet and pushed the tote bags aside, reaching for the tackle box. If I had something to hide from Mom, I'd definitely put it in a tackle box. I hoisted it out of the closet—it was a lot heavier than I expected. I plopped it on the ground and unsnapped the lid.

The top layer held lures and other fishing essentials—some line, some bobs, some other junk I couldn't identify. I slid the top shelf up and back on its hinges, revealing a larger compartment. More fishing crap, including a knife, an old rag, some scissors and... a little brown lunch bag.

My breath caught for a second, then I exhaled. I removed the bag with two fingers, as if it was contaminated with toxic waste.

The blood seemed to rush faster through my veins. It wasn't too late; I could still put everything back the way it was and slink off to my room. Sure, I wouldn't know Jason's plans with my mom, but I wouldn't have invaded his privacy either. Then I could be truly surprised when Mom flashed me the ring and told me she'd gotten engaged.

In my head, Miller's voice piped up. *Come on, chickenshit! Open the bag. See what the heck is going on. It's your freaking duty, compadre!*

I was pretty sure listening to Miller's advice was a bad long-term strategy, but I opened the bag anyway.

The bag contained a box. But it wasn't one of those little square boxes rings normally came in. It was a rectangular tin box. I pried open the tight-fitting top with my fingernails.

A small vial of white powder next to a little baggie of assorted pills in a variety of colors.

Oh man. Oh man oh man oh man. Jason was a doper. A million thoughts flooded my mind, but the loudest was: *I wonder if Mom knows.*

I closed the box and stuffed it back into the bag. In my haste to stuff the bag back into the tackle box, my hand grazed a rag and felt something hard beneath. Did Jason have more hidden secrets, along with his drugs?

I'd come this far, couldn't walk away now. I reached down and grabbed the rag and whatever it was concealing. My hands trembled, although I'd seen too many movies not to have a pretty good guess what might be hidden in the old oily t-shirt.

Very, very carefully, I unwrapped Jason's handgun.

Holy fuck.

Chapter Twenty

Quickly, I rewrapped the gun and wedged it back into the bottom of the tackle box. Adjusted the rag a few times, trying to get it exactly like I'd found it. Man, I should've taken a picture of it all.

I maneuvered the tackle box back into the closet and tried to remember how the tote bags had been arranged, hands shaking as I piled them on top. Had I returned everything to its proper place? Would Jason be able to tell I'd been rooting around? Did he have some kind of alarm system or nanny-cam in place protecting his stash?

Panic spread through my body as I stared at the stuff in the closet. Was the box in the right position? I moved it a little to the right. Better? Or worse? Were the tote bags piled in just the right way? I sucked in a deep breath and willed myself to calm down. I was being ridiculous. Jason wore shirts with spaghetti stains on them. He wasn't going to notice if his junk had moved three millimeters from where he'd left it. Was he? My thoughts wavered. I know I'd be more concerned about my illegal crap than about my appearance. Maybe he would be, too.

I gently closed the closet door and rushed to my room. Flopping on the bed, the impact of what I'd seen hit me. Mom had fallen in love with a low-life, gun-toting druggie.

I wondered if she knew.

* * *

I spent the afternoon holed up in my room trying to sort things out. Ever since I could remember, Mom had seized every opportunity to lecture me about the dangers of using drugs, even launching into vehement anti-drug tirades on occasion. And it wasn't just drugs she abhorred. She detested cigarettes, too, and she always read me all the DUI police reports from the newspaper. But I guess people had their inconsistencies—Jason smoked, and she put up with that. And she did like her white wine.

To me, though, drugs seemed like a whole other thing. Especially after what that doped-up driver did to my father.

And what about the pistol? Again, if I replayed all of Mom's lectures, I'd hear plenty of rants against guns. But, here, in reality, she allowed Jason to keep his hunting rifles in the basement. So which was it? Guns, bad? Or guns, depends?

My head hurt from all the contradictions bouncing around in there, slamming off the walls of my skull. Why couldn't people be as simple as the insects in the cages of Mom's menagerie? Eat, defecate, procreate. That's pretty much what occupied their little insectoid minds. They didn't have to worry about the loser their mother was about to marry.

I needed to figure out what to do. Of course, it would help a lot if *I* knew what *Mom* knew about Jason's hobbies. I tried to come up with a scenario in which she knew about them but was cool about the whole thing. Hard to believe. Mom wasn't exactly the type to shrink into a corner, shrug her shoulders, and say "whatever." If Mom didn't approve of something, she'd let you know—loud and clear.

I thought I could safely assume my mom wouldn't let Jason keep drugs and a gun in the house if she knew about it. So what should I do?

Several options sprang to mind. I could march back in there, grab the illegal items, and toss them in the nearest lake. Then pretend like nothing ever happened and try to hold in my smirks when Jason wandered around the house with a perplexed expression. But he'd probably just get me to drive him back to Stizzo or Razzo or Spazzy in Rockville and buy more drugs. Plus, he'd certainly be much more vigilant in keeping his stuff away from prying eyes in the future.

My thoughts turned darker. Jason struck me as the kind of guy who would be plenty pissed if he knew you went through his belongings, much less swiped them. I imagined him cornering me in the living room, threatening to disembowel me unless I confessed to stealing his stuff.

Taking his things was definitely out.

I could set a fire in the closet, but that seemed like overkill.

I could flat out tell her. *"Mom, have a seat. I've got some bad news. It's about Jason..."* Finding out about the drugs and the gun would crush her. I was pretty sure I didn't want to be the bearer of that bad news. I'd be forever associated with a rotten chapter in her life.

I could do nothing. Simply forget what I'd seen and go on treating Jason like I always had—with subtle disdain. But it wouldn't be fair to Mom. I knew she would be better off knowing the truth about Jason. At least in the long run. In the short run, it was anybody's guess how wrecked Mom would be. She was usually fairly resilient, but...

Nothing good was coming to me. Against my better judgment, I decided to seek some advice.

* * *

Twenty minutes later, I sat in Miller's bedroom. It was just as messy as before, but somehow it looked completely different, as if a backhoe had come through and churned up the layers of debris, like they do at landfills.

I explained the situation and outlined my lame options, complete with the possible outcomes as I saw them. Miller sat through the entire recounting with his eyes wide and his mouth shut—a first for him. When I finished, he broke his silence, the words practically bursting from his lips. "Holy shit. Right under your nose. Drugs, a gun. What kind of gun was it?"

"A handgun. You know, it had one of those cylinder things that spin around." I sighed again. I'd been sighing a lot since I closed Jason's closet door. "What am I going to do?"

"How about this? We call the cops and leave an anonymous tip. Then they raid your house, find the stuff, and haul Jason away to jail. All your problems are solved."

"Yeah, right. And have my mom taken in too, for conspiracy or harboring a fugitive or whatever? I don't think so."

"Maybe there'd be a gun battle. And Jason could get shot or something. You'd be a celebrity at school. And..." He paused and winked at me. "You'd get tons of chicks."

Even when the stakes were dead serious, Miller could be an ass. "Yeah, well, I'll forego getting laid so my house doesn't have to get shot up and my mom's boyfriend doesn't have to die."

Miller nodded sagely. "You are a stronger man than I."

"Who isn't?" I sighed again. "Come on, be serious. I've got to figure something out. I can't just tell Mom, can I?"

"As you may or may not know, I snoop on my sisters all the time. And I never rat them out to my parents. Not cool. I use whatever incriminating stuff I find as leverage."

"You mean blackmail?"

"I prefer 'leverage.' I get them to drive me places or give me things or look the other way when I need them to. I wash their hands, they scratch my back. Leverage."

"I think you're missing the point here. I don't want anything from

Jason. Except for him to be gone. I want to protect my mother from marrying a scumbag."

"And you don't want a scumbag for a step-dad, of course," Miller added.

"Of course. But this isn't about me. Really."

Miller's eyebrows arched, but he didn't say the obvious.

"Okay. So maybe it's about me...a little."

He just stared at me, lips pressed tightly together.

"Eff you, Miller."

His face turned serious. "Hey, what about fingerprints?

"What do you mean?"

"Did you leave your fingerprints on the gun? If something ever happens, the cops'll be knocking on your door in the middle of the night."

"I don't think I have to worry. My fingerprints aren't on file anywhere."

"Not yet, my friend. Not yet," Miller said. "Why do you think Jason has a gun, anyway?"

"How the hell should I know?"

"Maybe he's an undercover cop."

"Looking to infiltrate my family? What, he thinks my mom is using pesticides illegally? Get real."

"Maybe he just likes guns." Miller shrugged. "And drugs."

"You're not helping."

"Oh shit." Miller's head snapped up.

"What?"

"Well...nothing." His gaze flitted about his room, not settling on anything.

"What? What's 'oh shit'?"

"It's just..." An apologetic look appeared on Miller's face. "Well, maybe your mom knows about the drugs, and she..."

"Uses drugs? My mother? I don't think so."

"I know she's your mom and all, but…well, she is an adult, and sometimes kids don't always know what's going on with their parents."

The way Miller said it made me think he'd discovered something embarrassing about one of his own parents. But he didn't elaborate, and I didn't pursue it. "You're full of shit."

"You've got to admit it's *possible*. I mean anything's *possible*."

I shook my head. "That is *impossible*."

"Why is it so *impossible* anyway? She's only human." Miller was a born devil's advocate.

"I'll tell you why," I said, heart starting to beat faster. "Because my father died due to drugs."

Miller's face went pale.

"*He* wasn't using drugs. He was killed by a driver who was." I licked my lips and took a deep breath. "Some newbie driver got high, ran a stop sign, and slammed into my father."

"I'm sorry, Nick. I didn't mean to…" Miller chewed on his upper lip. "How come you never told me that before?"

I shrugged. "Now you know."

My father's fatal accident was my other dark secret, in addition to Uncle Steve's death. I'd kept it to myself for so long, it felt pretty good to tell someone, even if that person was Miller. Whenever someone had asked about my father, I'd always mumbled a vague explanation. People usually got the hint not to ask any more questions about it. But I guess I was maturing—or maybe it was just the dire situation with Jason that put things in a different perspective.

"I'm glad you told me. I have a tendency to say stupid things sometimes, so if I ever said something inappropriate about car accidents or stoned drivers or whatever, I apologize."

An apology? From Miller? This *was* a day to unburden special feelings. "Forget it. You didn't know. But that's why I'm sure my mom wouldn't do drugs or put up with someone who did."

Miller nodded, and he looked about as sincere as I'd ever seen him.

I didn't have anything to add, so we sat there, like a couple of statues, neither knowing how to move past the awkward, emotional moment we'd just shared.

Suddenly, Miller's face lit up. "Hey, this could be terrific news."

I didn't see how finding out my stepdad-to-be has a gun and uses drugs could be terrific news, but then again, I didn't usually share Miller's odd take on things. "Okay, I'll bite. How could this be good?"

"That engagement ring you thought he had wasn't an engagement ring. Maybe he's *not* going to marry your mom." He nodded once, proud of himself for delivering such great news.

"That's not making me feel any better. He'll pop the question sometime, I can tell. Ring or no ring, I'm screwed." This was getting to be too much. I needed to forget about Jason for a while, clear my head. Think about something more mundane. "What's the latest word on your parents' threat to send you off to boarding school?"

Now it was Miller's turn to sigh. "The same. I promised them I'd behave more and get my homework done, but..." He held his hands out, palms up.

"But they don't believe you? Shocking."

"I try, Nick. I try. But I'm a free-wheeling spirit." He cleared his throat. "Anyway, now I'm *really* going to try. My back's up against the fence, and the grass isn't looking too green. One thing I know—I'm definitely not cut out for military school."

"Finally, you said something that makes sense."

Miller cocked his head. "You know, I've been thinking. For both of us, this summer's been big. Full of challenges. Me with trying to get it together and convince my parents not to banish me, and you, with learning to swim and trying to get along with your stepdad-to-be and trying to get into Laura's pants." He paused to see my reaction, but I didn't give him the satisfaction. "Anyway, my question is this: Is this how life's going to be from now on? Full of turning points and challenges and big stuff happening?"

Every once in a while, some gem of insight managed to escape from the chaos in Miller's brain. "I suppose it is. I guess that's what makes life exciting."

Chapter Twenty-One

When I got home, Jason was watching TV in the family room. I wanted nothing to do with him, so I walked past, careful to keep my head down. I'd almost made it by when he called my name. "Hey, Nick. C'mere a sec."

I cursed my luck under my breath and entered the room. He thumbed the mute button on the remote, and Judge Judy fell silent. "Hey, Jason." I perched on a chair opposite the couch where he reclined.

"Whatcha been up to?" He pushed himself up to a sitting position.

"Nothing. Hanging out with Miller."

Jason nodded, eyeing me. "That all?"

I swallowed. "Yeah. Pretty much." My pulse started to pick up.

"You know who's got a pretty good bullshit detector?" He nodded at the TV. "Judge Judy. She can sniff out a liar."

"I guess." I glanced at the TV set. Some poor defendant was pleading her case and kept waving a piece of paper in the air and glaring at her opponent.

Jason cleared his throat, and I broke away from the screen. "Thirsty?" he asked, reaching behind the lamp to pull out a can of Sprite.

Oh shit, my Sprite! My heart stopped, and my eyes must have grown to the size of hubcaps. My jaw slowly hinged open. Like a photographic negative in my mind's eye, I saw my can of Sprite sitting atop Jason's dresser. *Right where I left it.*

"I asked if you were thirsty, Nick." Jason held up the can of Sprite and slowly turned it in his hand.

"Uh, no thanks. I'm good." My voice sounded small, as if I was talking from the bottom of a well.

"So, you hung out with Miller today. Sure you didn't do anything else worth mentioning?"

My mouth filled with cotton balls. Did he know what I found in his closet? "I, uh, well, I tutored this kid today. In math. And, uh, while he was here, he accidentally knocked over some of the insect cages, and they got loose. It was a real mess. So I had to scour the entire house catching the little buggers." As I got rolling, my voice got stronger. "I looked all over the house, downstairs. Even upstairs, in the bedrooms. Wanted to make sure I got them all."

"Uh huh." Jason didn't appear convinced. "And did you?"

"Did I what?"

"Get them all?"

"Oh. Uh, I think I did. Didn't see any upstairs, that's for sure."

"Good. You left your soda on my dresser." He held the green and silver can out to me.

"Oh. Sorry. I guess I forgot all about it during my bug hunt. I'll take care of it." Spotting my chance to clear out, I rose and reached for the Sprite. My fingers closed around the can, but Jason didn't let go. As I tried to pry it from his hand, he held on tighter.

"Listen, my man. I've moved in now, and I expect the same courtesy of privacy I give you." He locked eyes with mine, and I saw something there that made me shiver. "In other words, stay out of my stuff. Clear?"

I nodded. "Clear."

He released his grip on the can, and I pulled it away before he could grab it again and inflict me with more of his little lecture. "As long as we're on the same page."

"Got it."

He smirked and grabbed the remote, a signal we were finished. I turned to leave, and a second later, Judge Judy's grating voice filled the room as she ripped somebody a new one for trying to deceive her.

* * *

It had been an eventful day, and all the events had been bad. But there was one thing I'd wanted to do that I never got around to, what with all the bug-catching and contraband-discovering going on. I'd planned to ask Allie out.

It wasn't quite ten o'clock, but Mom and Jason had gone to bed. I'd been hunkered down in my room, watching YouTube videos for the last two hours. I picked up my phone. Text or call? Text or call? I decided on voice and tapped in Allie's number.

"Hello?"

"Uh, Allie? This is Nick. Nick Carlin."

"Oh, hi Nick. How are you?"

I imagined her radiant face getting brighter when she realized who was calling. "I'm good." No need to fill her in on how crappy my day had really been and ruin the moment, was there?

"Did you find any more bugs crawling around? So sorry about that. Colin can be a real...pain sometimes."

"I know, right? Don't worry about the bugs, I think we got them all."

"That's good." In the background, I heard her TV. "So, uh...?"

A vacuum in the room seemed to suck out all the air, and my tongue started to swell. If I didn't ask her now, I was afraid I'd wimp out. "Listen, I was wondering if I could, uh, you know, come over tomorrow or something."

"Come over tomorrow? Hang on a sec, okay?"

I heard her muffle the phone with her hand and ask somebody something, but I couldn't make out the words. It came through as

CHAPTER TWENTY-ONE

Blah Blah Blooh Blah, Blooh Blah.

My heart played jump rope while I waited for her answer.

"Nick? Tomorrow is fine. How about eleven?"

"I, uh, yeah, sure. Eleven sounds great." I paused, totally psyched, but surprised. Getting to go out with Allie had been a lot easier than I thought. Just pick up the phone, dial, and mission accomplished.

"Uh, Nick?" Allie's voice was louder.

"Yeah?"

"I said, 'See you tomorrow.'"

"Oh, right. See you tomorrow." I clicked off. At least today ended with a bang. I'd done it. I'd arranged some one-on-one hang-out time with Allie Merskie.

Things were looking up.

My stomach gurgled. I hadn't eaten much dinner, stressed as I was about my discovery. Time for a little late-night snack. If I recalled correctly, a couple of cold fried chicken drumsticks had my name on them.

I headed downstairs quietly, not wanting to wake Mom or Jason. I entered the kitchen and was about to flip on the overheads when I noticed the porch light on—and a shadowy figure pacing back and forth on the patio. I froze and watched through the sheer window curtains. Back and forth. Back and forth.

I grabbed the phone from its cradle, ready to dial 911, and crept to the back window, hunched over. As I got closer, some hushed words wafted through the window screen—as usual, Mom had left the window cracked open, just a hair, to let a little fresh air in.

It didn't take me long to identify the pacer—Jason, in a t-shirt and shorts. Talking on the phone, he paced back and forth like a large predatory cat at the zoo.

Was he making his call from outside just to be polite? Or had he gone outside so nobody would hear him talking to his drug dealer?

165

I snuck closer so I could make out his words.

"No. No, no, no. That's not what's going on," Jason said. He paused and kept on pacing, shaking his head at one point, undoubtedly in response to whatever was being said to him.

"Listen, Eve, it's not what you think. Have I ever lied to you?" he said, turning abruptly and switching directions. "You've always been my number one girl. You know that, right?"

What? Who the hell was Eve? The idea that Jason had another girlfriend somewhere—a number one girl—made me see red. What a total, complete asshole! My cheeks burned. I imagined myself popping out of my hiding place, barging out on the porch and catching Jason in the act of talking to Eve, and having him slink away, never to be heard from again. In the morning, when Mom asked me if I'd seen him, I'd just shrug and shake my head ambiguously. Sure, she'd be a wreck for a few weeks, but she'd get over it. Would that be better than knowing the truth?

Outside, Jason snorted. "Look, I told you. This isn't serious. I lost my job, couldn't make the rent, and I hooked up with her. I didn't have anyplace else to go, and I sure as shit didn't know you were moving back to town. Give me some time to square things up, okay? That's all I'm asking. You know you're the one I want to be with."

Would it be considered murder if I grabbed a kitchen knife and accidentally stabbed Jason a few dozen times? I bet I'd stand a fifty-fifty chance with a jury. Hell, Judge Judy would probably be on my side, if she could hear Jason's words.

"Come on, you're not being reasonable. I told you, I'll slip out of this thing as soon as I can. I've got some sense of responsibility, you know." Jason stopped moving and brought his free hand up to his head, as if he were holding the top of his scalp from blowing away. "I told you I'd do it, and I will. So fuck you." He whirled around and yanked open the kitchen door. He switched on the lights and saw me there, crouching under the window like the eavesdropper I was.

"The fuck you doing?"

I stood tall and took a step toward him. "Nothing. Came down for something to eat."

Jason licked his lips, breathing fast. "Yeah? How long you been there?"

"I just came down." My turn to glare at him. "Why?"

He met my stare. "I guess it goes back to the privacy issue we talked about today. I was making a private call. That's why I went outside. How much did you hear, anyway?"

"Enough." I resisted the urge to start whaling on him, although I was revved up enough to want to give it a go. But he was bigger and stronger than me, and a physical altercation between her son and her boyfriend was the last thing my mother needed. Well, second to last thing.

He tried to smile, but it came off looking way too forced. "Yeah, well, sometimes when you hear stuff out of context, it sounds worse than it is." He shrugged. "A friend's having a tough time, and I needed to give her some advice. She's really torn up, and it couldn't wait. You know, one of those end-of-the-world-as-I-know-it scenarios. Sorry if I gave you the wrong impression."

What was Miller's *rule* about wild-ass explanations? The longer and more detailed, the more full of shit the liar was? "Oh, what was her problem?"

Jason waved his hand as if he were swatting gnats. "Nothing that concerns you. In fact, it'd probably be best just to forget about the whole thing." He tried the fake smile again, then, when he realized it wasn't working on me, he replaced it with his customary scowl.

"Does this friend's *problem* concern Mom?"

His eyes flashed, and he lowered his voice, put some tough guy into it. "Not in the least. I don't know what's crawled up your ass, kid, and

I don't know what you're looking for exactly, but you can cut out the spying and snooping. I don't appreciate it, and I'm sure your mother wouldn't look kindly on how you're treating me." He poked me in the chest with his forefinger. "So quit eavesdropping and stop going through my stuff. You won't like what happens if you *really* piss me off." He punctuated his little tirade with another poke in the chest.

I stood my ground. I didn't respond, and I didn't even react to the pokes. He wasn't going to intimidate me. That wasn't quite true. He intimidated me plenty; I just wasn't going to give him the satisfaction of showing it.

With every ounce of willpower I could muster, I prevented myself from lashing out. Instead, I took a quick breath and brushed past him. He grabbed my arm from behind before I went three steps. He spun me around until his face was right in mine, cigarette breath and all. "One more thing. You don't want to upset your mother, do you? Then don't tell her what you *think* you heard tonight. You'd be wrong, and you'd be needlessly hurting her. Like I said before, you don't know the whole story here."

I wrested my arm from his grip. "Whatever. I'm not hungry anymore. I'm going to bed." I stormed out, without a glance back. I couldn't bear the thought of him seeing my tears.

Chapter Twenty-Two: T-minus 3 days

Gotta Grow Gills

The next morning, I was awakened by a *rat-a-tat-tat* on my bedroom door. If it was Jason, coming to tell me he'd decided to move out, then great. Otherwise, I wasn't thrilled about the intrusion. "Yeah?" I pulled the pillow over my head.

"Nick-o. You awake?" Mom opened the door. Light from the hallway spilled in, and I squeezed the pillow tighter over my eyes.

"I am now."

"Oh. Sorry. Come on, get up. Let's do some driving."

I moved the pillow just enough so I could see the clock. Ten minutes after seven. It wasn't Saturday, was it? "Now?"

"Yes, now. I think it would be a good idea for you to practice during a morning rush hour. And my first job today isn't until ten. I'll meet you in the kitchen in five minutes." She closed the door before I could complain.

I rolled out of bed and threw on some clothes, hit the bathroom, and shambled downstairs to the kitchen, eyes still half closed. Mom set a plate of scrambled eggs in front of me, along with a glass of orange juice. "Eat. Breakfast is the most important meal of the day, you know."

Although I wasn't a morning sunshine person, I usually possessed a healthy appetite. I wolfed down my breakfast in about ninety seconds. "Do we have to go driving today? Can't it wait until tomorrow?" The events of yesterday flooded back to me, and I was feeling pretty stressed and confused. Not exactly the right emotions to have as you fought rush hour for the first time.

"You've got to do it sometime. Might as well be now. Besides, who knows when I'll have the chance to do this again?"

I nodded, knowing when to cut my losses.

As we got underway, I had a tough time staying focused. I kept thinking back to what happened last night with Jason. Did I hear things right? Would he be leaving our lives soon? If so, part of me felt relieved, but I knew Mom would be devastated. On the other hand, if Jason was right and I had misunderstood what was going on, then *I* was going to be devastated. A sure no-win situation. I struggled to put my thoughts on hold while I drove.

The neighborhood roads proved no problem. But when we hit I-66, it was easy to tell why people called it rush hour. Traffic moved like sludge going eastbound, toward Washington. Thankfully, Mom suggested we start by going west. Traffic was heavy there, too, but not impossible. I merged into the stream of cars easily, then tried to maintain a steady 55 for a while. Mom paid closer attention to the speed limits than Jason had.

As we motored along, we got the usual stares from people who'd never seen a critter cruiser before. Some would shake their heads and laugh; a few looked as if they'd eaten silverfish for breakfast. After a while, I learned to ignore the gawkers.

"So, Nick-o, how are things going in your life?" Mom asked.

"Okay." Sometimes, fewer words were better. This qualified as one of those times.

"How's the social life?"

"Good." I considered telling Mom about going to Allie's later today, but I didn't want to open the floodgates for a billion questions.

"No details?" Mom rearranged herself in the seat to half-face me and half-face the road.

"Nope. Don't worry, I'll let you know when I get engaged."

"Funny." I sensed Mom tense up, as she pointed at a car in the next lane. "Watch out for him. I don't like the way he's driving."

He seemed to be driving okay to me, but I slowed to let him get ahead of us.

"Hey, what's this tutoring thing you've got going?"

"Just one kid. In math. No big deal, really."

"Well, I think it's great you took some initiative and went out and got a paying gig." She paused. "It does pay, doesn't it?"

"Yes, it pays."

"Well, then. That's good." Mom pointed out a truck lumbering along in the left lane. "I sure wish they'd do something about those trucks. Aren't they supposed to be in the right lanes?"

"You want them in our lane?"

"Well, not right now. In general. They should drive safer."

"Uh huh."

"Watch out!" About thirty feet ahead, a car cut into our lane, and Mom threw her arm in front of me, as if her arm was going to be more secure than the seat belt I was wearing.

"I see it." I tapped the brakes, just to make Mom happy, but the car wasn't even close. I really needed to learn how to swim so I could be out driving on my own, without Mom sitting next to me, stressed about every stupid thing.

Mom took her arm back. "Sorry. I get a little carried away, don't I? Let's change the subject. I talked to Gram last night and she said she needs you to help her with something."

"What?" As Miller would say, I needed more problems like I needed another hole in my ass.

"She wasn't too clear. I think it was some kind of computer thing. I'm still worried about her. She hasn't seemed like herself. She's been looking much older lately."

"She seems okay to me." I wondered if Mom knew about Herb and was afraid to bring up the topic, not wanting to paint an unflattering portrait of Gram.

"Yeah? Well, I don't know. Tell me if you see anything unusual, okay?"

Why did she have to say that every time we talked about Gram? Why did *everyone* think I was some kind of spy? "Sure, Mom. No sweat."

"Thanks. I know I can always count on you." She reached over and patted my shoulder. "How's the swimming going?"

Once Mom got stuck in inquisition mode, it was tough to knock her loose. "Fine. I guess. Although…"

"What?"

"I think I've proven to you how important I feel swimming is. I've taken all those lessons and I've practiced just about every day. I think you should let me get my license no matter what happens with the test."

"Now, Nick. We had an agree—"

"I'm not saying I won't take the swim test. I'm just saying that if—for some reason—I don't exactly pass, I should be able to get my license anyway."

"Come on, don't get started on this again. We have a deal."

"People can change deals, you know. Happens all the time." I eased off the accelerator. We'd crept up to about 65 mph. Mom was too busy being stubborn to notice.

"Well, it's not happening this time. You absolutely need to learn how to swim. Period. End of discussion." She folded her arms across her chest and stared out the windshield. "And, by the way, you should have more confidence in yourself. You should be thinking, 'I am *so* going to pass my test. I am *totally* going to ace it.' Not, 'if I don't pass then blah blah blah.'"

We drove in silence, and I stewed. I'd hit a wall with my swimming. Unless I got some divine intervention, I didn't think I had a shot of passing, self-confidence or not. "How about listening to the radio?" I hoped to preemptively stave off any more of Mom's interrogation.

"Nope. Not safe. Maybe when you're twenty." She grinned. "If you're real good, maybe when you're nineteen."

I grunted my disapproval.

"If I didn't know better, I'd think you didn't want to talk to me." She shifted in her seat again. "You know, I miss the time we spent together. We used to talk about everything. Now..."

Now you have a live-in boyfriend. A live-in *scumbag* boyfriend. "Come on, Mom. We still talk plenty."

"Hmm. I guess. Things must be a little bumpy for you right now. With Jason, I mean. Why don't you tell me how you're feeling about it all? You can tell me anything, just like old times."

For the briefest of moments, I debated telling her what I'd found in Jason's closet and what I'd overheard during his phone call. But I didn't have the strength to do that to my mom. Not now, anyway. Maybe after Jason screwed us over some more, I'd risk telling her. I glanced over into her expectant face. She was hoping—practically praying—I'd open up with my feelings. So far, I'd taken pains not to learn much about Jason and his past. Now, though, that information might help me interpret what I'd heard. "You're right. It's hard having someone new in our lives."

She nodded. "Go on."

"Where did you meet Jason, anyway?"

"I was at a party with Celia, and we met. It wasn't like in the movies where two people see each other across the crowded room and know they'll end up together. In our case, we just happened to both be in

173

line to use the bathroom. I thought I'd told you before, no?"

"Sorry, I don't remember. Hey, should we turn around?" Traffic on the other side of the highway had thinned, so I figured it was safe to head back. Get home and away from Mom's therapy session as soon as possible.

"Actually, I wanted to stop by that new outdoors store. Pick up something for Jason. They're having a grand opening sale."

What? Shit. "Do we have to do that now?"

"It's right on our way. In fact, it's the next exit."

Now I knew why we needed to go driving this particular morning, in this particular direction. "Can't you just—"

"Enough." Mom raised her voice and glared at me.

"Sorry." Maybe I should tell her about Jason now, before she bought his gift.

Mom softened her tone. "So, we were talking about Jason, weren't we?"

I didn't answer.

"I know you don't know much about him, but you'll get a chance to learn more. I know it's still a ways off, but we were thinking we'd fly out to spend Thanksgiving with his parents. In St. Louis."

"Oh?"

"Don't worry. You'd come, too." She patted me again. "Of course. I wouldn't spend Thanksgiving without you."

I wanted to say, "You might be spending Thanksgiving without Jason," but I settled for "What about Gram?" We'd spent every Thanksgiving I could remember with her. The day often ended with her drinking too much wine and butchering Christmas carols at high volume.

"Don't worry. We'll work something out." She sighed. "What can I do to help you and Jason get along better? Just name it, and it's done."

Dump him? Have him arrested? Cut off his balls? "I dunno. I guess it'll just take some time." I flipped on my turn signal and checked my rear-view mirror to make sure no lunatics were speeding along the shoulder heading for the exit. It was clear, so I slowed and left the highway. At the light, I turned right and followed Mom's directions toward the store.

"Well, I appreciate it, Nick-o. Jason means a lot to me—I really think things could work out. You know, for the duration."

"That's, uh, great, Mom." The urge to blurt out what I knew attacked me again, and I clenched my teeth to make sure I didn't spill. No good could come from telling Mom. I couldn't protect her from getting hurt badly—too late. Best thing I could do would be to ride out the storm and support her however I could.

We drove the rest of the way to the store in silence. Mom, probably deep in thought about her beloved Jason, and me, trying to come up with ways to comfort her when she had her heart ripped out.

Amazingly, I didn't crash on the way.

Chapter Twenty-Three

No matter how bad I felt about my mom's situation and by extension, my situation, I wasn't going to let it ruin my time with Allie. After we got home from driving, I took a shower and threw on some clean clothes. Not too fancy, but not too raggy, either. I was going for the casual cool look.

I rode my bike over, timing my arrival for eleven on the dot. I knocked on the door and took a deep breath. Two deep breaths, actually. After all, it *was* Allie Merskie.

Allie answered the door flashing her trademarked smile. "Hey, Nick. Right on time. Come on in." She wore a different pair of tight shorts and a baby blue t-shirt with the word *pink* stenciled in yellow letters.

I stepped into the foyer, and the smell of cookies greeted me. Chocolate chip, if my nose was any judge. And it was pretty good at identifying baked goods. My heart fluttered as I realized she'd baked them for me. For us. "Something smells good."

"Cookies," Allie said, smile bright as ever. "Hold on a sec." She walked over to the staircase and shouted, "Hey, Colin. Nick is here. Come on down."

Colin? Why is she calling Colin? I ran through the possibilities in my head but came up empty. Maybe she just thought it would be polite if he said hello.

She turned to me. "He'll be down in a minute. You know how he can be, right?"

"Uh, sure. So, what do you—" I stopped mid-sentence as a very large guy came striding across the foyer from someplace in the back. Wavy blond hair, muscles on muscles. His shirt stretched to cover his massive chest.

Allie's already beaming smile blossomed. The hulk returned it and came to a standstill next to her. He put his tree limb of an arm around her shoulder. "Hey," he said to me.

I felt like I was back in fifth grade when Anthony Petraglia socked me in the stomach and knocked the wind out of me. It took a lot, but I managed to force out a "hey" in return.

Allie introduced him. "This is Blake Harrison. He's my boyfriend."

Blake stuck out his grapefruit-sized fist for me to bump. I tapped knuckles, head spinning. *Boyfriend?*

"It's so nice of you to make time to tutor Colin," Allie said. "My parents appreciate it."

"And you have my sympathy, dude," Blake added. "Colin can't be an easy one to teach."

Allie mock-elbowed Blake in the gut. "Cut it out. I'll bet you were a handful too when you were his age."

Blake growled. "I'm still a handful." He tickled Allie, who started to giggle.

I felt like I'd already shrunk to the size of an ant. Maybe I should crawl away now before I got completely squashed.

"Cut it out," Allie said, and after one final tickle, Big Blake withdrew his paw. Allie glanced at me, standing there, shifting my weight back and forth between my feet. "Oh, let me get Colin."

"Hang on. I'll get him," Blake said. He took the stairs three at a time before Allie could say a word.

"He, uh, seems nice," I said.

"Oh, he's a doll. We're going to the same school. Virginia Tech."

Terrific. "That sounds nice."

"Yeah. In fact…" She looked at me, and her smile faded, replaced by something a little more sympathetic.

"What?"

"I'm sorry, Nick. We've decided to take a little vacation before heading to school. We leave tomorrow." She smiled again, but her heart wasn't in it. "I won't be able to give you any more swimming lessons. And I won't be there for your test. Don't worry, though. I'm sure you'll do fine. Just remember to breathe."

Squash.

The next thing I knew, Allie was grabbing my arm. "Nick, are you okay?"

"Uh, sure. I'm fine. I'm good."

Allie let go and stepped back. "You looked flushed for a moment. Like you were going to pass out or something."

"No, no. I'm okay. Just felt a touch queasy. Must have had some bad eggs for breakfast. Nothing to worry about."

She cocked her head. "Okay, then. Good."

Both of us turned as we heard rumbling on the stairs. Blake seemed to be helping Colin along with a not-so-gentle mitt on the shoulder.

"Okay, okay. Quit pushing. I'm going." Colin slid to a stop in his socks on the tile floor.

"Well, here's your pupil now," Allie said. "Colin, take Nick down to the study room. If you're good, I'll bring down a few fresh-baked chocolate chip cookies."

Colin opened his mouth to say something snide, but after a quick glance at Blake, changed his mind.

"Well, have fun, you two." Allie winked at me, then escorted Blake—arm-in-arm—toward the kitchen and the cookies. *Our* cookies.

Colin glared at me. Tutoring him was the last thing I wanted to do, but I couldn't back out. Not without admitting why I'd come in the first place. And I'd rather tutor a dozen Colins than own up to that stupidity. "Ready for some math?" I asked.

Colin snarled. "Stuff it. I might have to do this, but I don't have to like it."

Neither did I. Even the prospect of thirty bucks didn't help ease the pain.

* * *

As I was finishing up with Colin—and he'd been just as cooperative as he had in the past—I got a call from Gram. She wanted to know if I could come over and help her with something. Why not? I had nothing else going on. I told her I'd be there in a few minutes.

I said goodbye to Allie and Blake and wished them good luck with school. Allie gave me a goodbye hug and an extra chocolate chip cookie for the road.

On the bike ride to Gram's, I came to two conclusions. One, I wasn't having a very good week. For that matter, I wasn't having a very good summer. And two, I was tired of riding my crappy bike around—I needed to pass that damn swimming test.

When I got to Gram's, I noticed only one Taurus in the driveway. She ushered me into the sunroom and offered me a glass of lemonade and some chocolate chip cookies. Hers were from a Chips Ahoy bag, but I took a few just to be polite. At least they weren't from her Judith.

"So, what's wrong with your computer, Gram?" I asked after downing about half the glass of lemonade.

"My computer? Nothing, I hope." She perched on the edge of her chair, just waiting to swoop in and gather up any stray crumbs. I bit into one of the cookies very carefully and chewed with my mouth closed.

I swallowed. "I thought Mom said you had a computer problem."

179

"Not me. Must be her other mother. I do have something I'd like to discuss with you, though. Two things, actually."

"Fire away."

"Well, you remember Herb, right? The fella you met the other day?" She examined my face, probably to see my reaction to her boyfriend's name. I tried to keep neutral.

"Of course, Gram. I remember Herb. I don't usually forget people I move furniture with."

"Uh-huh. Well, I like him. He's a sweet man. But…" She shrugged.

"But what?" I took a sip of lemonade.

Gram considered her words. "I need to cut him loose."

I snorted, and some lemonade went up my nose. It reminded me of getting a shot of chlorine. Neither was a pleasant sensation.

"Oh my. Are you okay?"

Why was everyone asking me that today? I tried to get it together. "Yeah, I'm fine. Why do you need to cut Herb loose?"

"Well, Herb is smart and funny and handsome, but…" Gram paused again, and I wondered if we were playing some kind of fill-in-the-blank game.

"But what?" I put down my glass.

"The sex stinks."

I blinked a few times, trying to maintain my poker face.

She eyed me. "You know sex is important in a relationship, right?"

"Sure, Gram."

"Herb just doesn't have what it takes, I'm afraid."

Didn't they have little blue pills for that? "That's, uh, too bad."

"Yes, it is. So, how should I do it?"

"Do it?"

"Cut him loose. Show him the door. Hosta la vista, Herbie."

Gram was asking break-up advice from me? "Just tell him it's not working out. It's been nice, but…" I shrugged. "You could always say 'it's not you, it's me.'"

She leaned back and seemed to ponder my suggestions. "'It's not you, it's me.' Isn't that kind of lame?"

I shrugged. "I guess. But it might be better than the truth, in this case. Nobody wants to hear…" I stopped, unable to say what I was thinking. My grandmother!

Gram had moved on. "I had such a wonderful relationship with your grandfather—in all ways. He was so vigorous in the bedroom. And he was my true soulmate. I guess, it's just…" She stopped talking and dabbed at her eyes with a tissue she'd been hiding in her dress.

"No one can live up to him," I finished for her.

She nodded, and the tears started to flow more freely. Why had she decided to talk to *me* about this? Instead of Mom? Boys my age weren't usually thought of as good listeners. I guess I was honored, anyway.

"I just…" She kept sobbing and pulled another tissue from thin air. Blew her nose into it.

I kept quiet and waited. At some point, the faucet had to stop dripping, didn't it?

Gram blew her nose once more, a huge blast, then seemed to recover. "I just wish I'd have been a little more adventurous before I settled down." She glanced at me. "You know?"

I had the sense this conversation was about to take a sharp left into the weeds. "Uh, Gram, I'm not so sure I—"

"Sex, Nick. I'm talking about sex. You know what I'm talking about, right?"

"Yes, well, do you think I'm the one you should be talking to about this?" I picked up my glass of lemonade as if to say I was done with this topic.

"Oh, pshaw. I'm sure your mother gave you the Talk years ago." Gram leaned forward. "There's nothing bad about good sex. I just wish I'd had more of it when I was young and could really enjoy it."

"So, uh, what was the problem you needed help with, Gram?"

"It's just a shame. I wish I knew then what I know now." Her expression took on a faraway cast, and I knew I was in trouble. No derailing this train.

I grabbed another cookie from the box, leaned back on the sofa, and waited for Gram's lament to run its course.

"I would have had much more sex. And been more adventurous. With many different people. You only live once, and when you get to be my age, you realize there's not that much time left. You start thinking about all the things you never did." She raised her voice and jabbed her finger in the air. "And, by gum, that includes all the sexual things I never did, too."

I tried to think of a tune in my head so I wouldn't have to hear any more disgusting details of Gram's sexual desires. Too much more of this, and I was going to seriously consider becoming a monk. "Gram. Come on, don't feel bad about the stuff you haven't done. Be grateful for the stuff you *have* done." *Just don't tell me about that, either.*

She nodded. "Oh, I am. I am. A wonderful daughter and a doubly wonderful grandson. I am truly blessed. But..."

No fill-in-the-blank answer came to mind, so I simply stared at her.

"I'm trying to pass along this bit of wisdom to you, Nick. If you see something you want, go for it. Don't be shy, don't hesitate, don't always question yourself. Take the bull by the horns and go after what you want. Regret sucks."

"Uh, thanks, Gram. I'll take that lesson to heart."

She waved her hand at me. "I know, I know, I'm just a doddering old fool. Well, you can blow smoke up my skirt if you like, but I'm shooting straight with you." She smiled at me. "I love you, Nick. I'm just trying to give you a few tips about happiness."

"Thanks. And I really mean it." I imagined the line I'd be giving the next girl I met at a party. *"Hey, we should hook up. My grandmother says*

I should go for all the action I can get!"

"What are you smiling about?"

"Oh, nothing." I wiped the smirk from my face. "You sure you don't have any other problems that need fixing?"

"There is something else I wanted to tell you." Suddenly, the tears were gone, and her face was bright again. "Come with me."

She rose and glided from the room. I followed her to the front window in the living room. She pulled back the curtains and pointed. "See the car in the driveway?"

I peered through the gap in the curtains. Her brown Taurus was the only vehicle out there. "Your car. Is it giving you problems?"

"Nope. Runs like a dream. I don't really drive it very far, though."

"Okay."

"Nick, I want to give it to you. When you get your license, I mean." She turned, and I spotted a few tears in her eyes, but this time they weren't sad ones.

It was a generous offer, but I didn't think I could snatch my grandmother's car right out from under her, even if she was okay with it. "Thanks. Thanks a lot. But I can't accept it. How are you going to get around?"

"Don't worry about me, Nicky boy. I've been thinking about getting a new car. A sports car. A hot red convertible." She winked at me. "That'll attract some studs, don't you think?"

"I can't take your car, Gram."

"It's not polite to refuse gifts. Especially from your grandmother. I want you to have it. You'll enjoy it a lot more than I will."

I nodded. That was probably true. Even though it wasn't a hot car, it was tons better than driving the Bugmobile. I certainly wouldn't get as many crazy looks. "I don't know. What will Mom say?"

"She'll say whatever I tell her to say. And I'll tell her to say it's okay." She snaked her arm around my waist. "Please let an old lady do something nice for her favorite person in the whole world. Please, Nicky." She squeezed me harder.

Well, when you put it that way. "Okay. Sure. I mean, wow, Gram, my own car! Thank you, thank you, thank you."

I looked out the window again at the car. *My* car.

Chapter Twenty-Four

Gram fed me grilled cheese sandwiches for lunch—along with a few more chocolate chip cookies for dessert—and I said goodbye. I hopped on my bike thinking this could be one of the last times I'd be riding it around town—as a mode for transportation anyway. I supposed I might still ride it for fun or exercise or…nah, who was I kidding? As soon as I got my license—and my car—the bike would go straight into the shed.

Instead of biking home, I rode around Gram's block. Then I stopped up the street, making sure I was hidden from sight in case she peered out the window. I set the bike down and sat on the curb where I could see my car.

My own car. I could hear Miller now, oohing and aahing. He'd probably make a few cracks about it being an old-lady car, at the same time he was salivating on the bumpers. It wasn't the car itself that was so great—heck, it *was* kind of an old-lady car. It was the freedom. No longer would I have to rely on Mom and the availability of the Bugmobile. I'd be able to go where I wanted, when I wanted. More importantly, I'd be able to go out with girls and not gross them out driving around in a car that transported bugs or rodents or snakes. Definitely a buzzkill.

Of course, one thing stood in my way. The swimming test.

My chance of passing had taken a hit when I found out Allie wouldn't be around to cheer me on. What was I going to do? I had the fundamentals down, but when it came to putting everything together, when I got to the point when I actually started to believe I could swim, I'd fallen apart. Maybe Laura was right, maybe I had some sort of mental blockage. Afraid of failure?

Laura.

I could ask Laura for help. She'd offered. She'd been on the swim team. She was a good friend. I kept staring at the Taurus. *My* Taurus. Gram's words echoed in my head. *Go after what you want. Regret sucks.*

Maybe Laura could teach me a few things. I pulled out my phone and texted her, asking if she could meet me at the pool later that afternoon. *I need your help. Can you teach me to swim? Pretty please?*

Sure, my pleasure.

I stowed the phone and got back on my bike. Headed home. During the entire ride back, I thought about Gram's advice. *Regret sucks.*

* * *

I arrived at the pool before Laura, so I grabbed a chaise lounge and waited. It was getting late in the season, and there didn't seem to be as many people as usual—maybe they'd all decided to cram their restful vacations into the last two weeks of August.

Every time PZ scuffled by, I closed my eyes, pretending I was asleep. I could still feel her laser stare right through my eyelids.

When Laura came strolling onto the pool deck, all the other girls faded into the background. Tanned and lithe in her black two-piece, I wondered how in the world I was ever going to be able to concentrate on swimming. Then I pictured her—still in her bikini—in the front seat of my Taurus, and my thoughts turned back to swimming. Mostly.

"Hey, Nick." She plopped her pool bag down on the chaise next to mine. "How's my little minnow today?"

"Minnow?"

"That's what we used to call the little kids who couldn't swim. Actually, those were the ones with promise. The hopeless ones we called pebbles."

"So I have promise?"

"Well, maybe I spoke too soon. Come on, show me what you've got."

We jumped into the pool, and after a few minutes of playful splashing around, Laura got serious. "Why don't we run you through the fundamentals to see if there are any, uh, deficiencies. Remember, you need a solid foundation to build a strong house."

I kicked and I stroked. I breathed and I blew. As I completed each skill, she nodded and offered encouragement. A couple times, she put her hands on my back or my arms, helping to guide me into the correct positions. I didn't mind the assistance one bit.

For my part, I tried to remain focused so I could ace every single test. I really wanted to impress my teacher. And, of course, I wanted to learn how to swim.

"Wow. I'd say you've got all the components down pat," she said, actually *seeming* impressed. "Let's see how well you put them all together."

The moment of truth. I took a deep breath and pushed off from the wall. Stretching my body to its full extension, I tried to become one with the water. I glided along for a moment, then began stroking. Right arm out of the water, stretch, into the water, pull down. Left arm out of the water, stretch, into the water, pull down. Kick, kick, kick. My heart raced as I realized I was moving forward. I was swimming.

I repeated the sequence. And again. But I'd taken too many strokes without a breath. I turned my head and opened my mouth and swallowed half the pool. My arms stopped stroking, my legs stopped kicking. I stopped swimming. Standing on the bottom of the pool, I glanced back at Laura, still by the side. She gave me a lackluster round of applause and motioned me back.

Not confident I could even dogpaddle back, I walked—slowly—to where she stood.

"Not bad, not bad. You had it going there for a minute." She wiped some spray from her face. "I think the whole breathing thing is messing you up."

Duh. "So what's the solution?"

"Keep on trying."

We spent the next thirty minutes trying. I tried with nose plugs and without, with goggles and without, and we even tried it with *Laura* wearing goggles and nose plugs while she watched me. Nothing worked. I'd get it going for a while, and then things would go south in a hurry. No matter what I tried doing, or what I tried thinking, nothing seemed to do the trick. I think I'd easily become Laura's worst swimming pupil ever in record time. What was worse than being a *pebble*?

Finally, Laura threw her hands up. "Enough. Time to take a break."

We regrouped on the lounge chairs. Laura wrapped a towel around her, while I decided to let the sun dry me. "See. I told you I was a swimming reject."

Laura stared at me, squinting against the sun. She appeared to be reading something on my face, as if I had the answer to why I couldn't swim scrawled on my forehead. I swiped the back of my hand across my nose, just in case she was staring at a booger instead of trying to read me. "No, I don't think you're a swimming reject. A regular reject maybe, but not a swimming reject." She grinned.

It was my turn to try to read her. Staring at her face, only one thought came to mind. I wanted to lean over and kiss her on the lips. A shiver rippled up from my toes straight into my groin, despite the warmth from the sun. "So, uh, what do you think my problem is?"

"Do you trust me, Nick?"

"Sure. Of course." I'd known her for years, and she was one of my best friends. I trusted her totally, despite her recent *friendship* with Air Force.

"Then come with me." She gathered up her stuff and grabbed my hand, not wasting a minute. We had to split up so we could exit through our respective locker rooms, but we rejoined outside the pool.

"Where are we going?"

She held a finger up to her lips. "Ask no questions, grasshopper. You shall be enlightened."

"Okay." A while had passed since I'd last been enlightened.

"How did you get here?" she asked.

I pointed to my bike sitting in the rack across the parking lot. "Rode. You?"

"Walked. Can we both fit on your bike?"

"Worth a try." It had been years since I'd ridden someone else on my bike, but I was willing to give it a shot. Especially with Laura.

It took us a few minutes to figure out how to do it, but eventually we got her halfway on the middle bar with her legs dangling over the handlebars. It didn't look very comfortable, but she claimed she was okay. And she said we weren't going very far.

She directed me along the neighborhood streets. Having her so close to me was distracting, and if I didn't know better, I'd say I was even a bit lightheaded. She'd put a long t-shirt over her bikini, but it rode up every so often, and I got an up-close-and-personal view of her perfect thighs. I tried to keep my eyes on the road so we wouldn't crash; it was one of the most difficult things I'd ever had to do.

I could tell our destination well before we got there, although I didn't say anything, figuring it would be rude to ruin her surprise. We turned into the small parking lot near the basketball courts, then wound our way along the asphalt path to the little dock overlooking our pond.

I came to a stop and helped her off the bike, then ditched it on the grass next to the path. We walked to the end of the fishing dock and leaned over the rail facing the pond, shoulder-to-shoulder, just as we'd done scores of times in the past. This time, though, there was an additional charge of electricity in the air. I wondered if Laura felt it, too.

"So, this is where I'm going to get enlightened?" I tried to get a glimpse of her face in my peripheral vision.

"That's the plan, Stan."

"Can I ask you a question first?"

"I guess it depends on the question."

The breeze picked up, and I caught a whiff of her coconutty sunscreen. Funny, I didn't recall smelling it when she was practically sitting in my lap on the bike. "How's it going with Air Force?"

I heard her draw in a breath, then let it out. Not quite a sigh, but not a happy sound either. "He's a nice guy and all, but…he's a little too much into himself, if you know what I mean."

My heart skipped. I knew exactly what she meant. I also knew what her statement meant for me. I had an opening. *Don't screw this up.* "So you and him…?"

"There is no me and him." She forced a smile. "Forget it. We've got more important stuff to discuss. I've been thinking about your swimming situation."

I'm not sure I'd say that was more important than Laura's status, but I wasn't going to press the issue. I refocused on the here and now. "Okay. What about my swimming? Or lack thereof?"

She turned toward me and screwed her face up, as if she were preparing to explain Einstein's Theory of Relativity to a first grader. "Like I told you before, I think it's a mental thing."

I started to roll my eyes but caught myself in time. "I want to learn how to swim. I'm trying to learn how to swim. Very hard, in fact."

"Hear me out, Nick. And try to keep an open mind, okay?" She took

190

my hands in hers. We were standing inches apart, holding hands. The sun was shining, the birds were chirping, beautiful nature surrounded us. And all I wanted to do was rip off our clothes and let nature take over. Of course, I'd settle for a single kiss. *How's that for an open mind?*

I managed to squeak out an "okay."

"Remember a field trip we took in eighth grade? To the Kennedy Center?"

"Yeah. I think so."

"Remember what happened on the ride home?"

I searched my memory banks, came up empty. "Not really."

Laura nodded knowingly, like she'd been expecting me to draw a blank. "You don't remember seeing the accident?"

I closed my eyes and tried again. Tried to jostle some long-forgotten memory. A few snatches of some images shimmered behind my eyes. Maybe. Maybe not. I shook my head slowly.

"We were driving home, on the bus, and we saw an accident on the other side of the road. A car had gotten mashed up pretty bad. There was an ambulance, and we could see them hauling out the body." Her grip on my hands tightened.

"Okay. So?"

"I was sitting next to you, and all the color drained from your face. You looked like a ghost or something." She paused, evidently waiting for me to say something, to confirm her memory. Unfortunately, I couldn't.

"And?"

"You told me about your father. It was the first time you'd ever mentioned any details. About how he'd been killed by a guy who'd been driving high." She took a deep breath. "You were pretty upset and made me promise not to tell anyone. Ever. You didn't even want me to mention it to you again."

Now that she recounted what had happened, the watery memory

sharpened in focus, but I still didn't recall the events clearly. Although the "making her promise" part *did* sound like something I'd insist on. "I'm getting a vague recollection of something. What does this have to do with swimming?"

She tilted her head up slightly, and her features softened. "When you told me about the terrible tragedy, you were trembling. Kind of like how you are now."

She let go of my hands, and the tremors became more pronounced. Herky-jerky motions I couldn't control. I hadn't even been aware of them. I jammed my hands in my pockets and looked away, insides starting to churn.

"It's okay, Nick. Maybe you need to let it out. Talk it over some more."

"Who are you, Dr. Phil?"

"Better than Dr. Phil. I'm your friend. One of your best friends. I want to help you."

"Well, I appreciate the help, but I don't see how talking about what happened to my dad will help. It just makes me sad."

"What happened is sad. Tragic. But if you let it mess you up, it becomes even more tragic." She exhaled, and her minty breath seemed out of place on the fishing dock. "Sometimes a best friend can see things you can't. And I believe it's a best friend's duty to help."

How about we go home and forget this conversation happened? I kept my gaze focused on a few tree stumps along the far bank of the pond.

Laura reached up and touched my chin with a finger. Slowly, she turned my face toward her. In a steady voice, she said, "Nick, I think you're not learning to swim because you're afraid of getting your license. Then you'll be a young driver. Just like the guy who killed your father."

The sounds of nature gradually quieted, as if someone had slid the volume control slowly to zero. *I couldn't swim because I was scared to get my license?* Was there anything behind Laura's theory? Was I afraid to get my license? Afraid I'd become the asshole who my mother hated with all her heart, still to this day? I didn't usually subscribe to psychological mumbo-jumbo like this—no matter how much Miller insisted it was real—but why *couldn't* I learn how to swim?

I suppose it was possible. Hell, *anything* was possible.

I leaned back against the dock rail, staring into the woods behind the pond, but not really seeing anything. Laura stood on my right, without moving, barely breathing, probably worried my head would implode or something as I tried to absorb what she was suggesting.

On some level, her theory made sense. The most traumatic event in my life logically would have a great effect on my behavior—if not outright then subconsciously.

It was funny. When I was a younger kid, taking all those lessons, Mom figured it was Uncle Steve's drowning that made me skittish in the water. And she was probably right. We'd had a ready-made excuse that had turned into a self-fulfilling prophecy.

Now, when I really wanted to swim, I thought I'd been able to put the drowning story behind me—not totally, but enough to get into the water—only to be derailed by my subconscious. Tricky thing, the mind.

One other thing occurred to me. Maybe on some level, I didn't want to stress Mom out by getting my license. Then I'd be on the road, susceptible to what happened to my father. If I never got my license, I couldn't very well get rammed by another car while out driving myself around.

I turned to Laura. "Say you're right about this. What difference does it make? I still can't swim."

"Now that you know what's holding you back, you'll figure it out." She took my hands again and squeezed them. "You're a good driver.

You don't do drugs. There's absolutely no reason to think you'll be like that other kid. Absolutely none. I'd trust you with my life, Nick." A faint smile appeared on her lips, then vanished. "And I can't say that about most people I know."

A weird warmth spread its way from my hands, up my arms, into my torso, down into my legs. Could it be that Laura's insight had freed my spastic swimming muscles? If not physically, at least psychologically? Would I be able to overcome my subconscious barrier, now that I knew I had one and what it was? Wasn't there some kind of saying that it's better to "face the devil you know than the one you don't"? Too many questions, not enough answers.

"Nick?" Laura stared at me, unblinking.

"Huh?"

"You can do this. I know you can. I've seen you in the water. You've got the skills. You just have to believe in yourself. I believe in you. If you set your mind to it, I know you'll do it. For an absolute certainty. And I'm always right about stuff like this."

"I hope so. I really hope so." I wanted to lean over and kiss her, right on her inviting lips, but something held me back. Maybe after I got my license.

Chapter Twenty-Five: T-minus 12 hours

Oh Man Oh Man Oh Man Oh Man!

It was Friday night, the night before my big swimming test, and Miller, Johnny B, and I were leaning against the American Eagle Outfitters display window. We'd been there for about five minutes after having cruised the entire mall, twice, without finding any other group of guys—or girls—to glom onto.

"How was computer camp?" I asked Johnny B.

"Bunch of nerds."

"So you were right at home," Miller said, putting his arm up to deflect Johnny B's punch, if it came.

"Funny man," Johnny B said. "I've had enough camps this summer to last me for years."

"At least they're better than military school." Miller's face sagged, while Johnny B and I exchanged glances.

No one said anything for a moment, then Johnny B cleared his throat. "Okay, I guess it's time. Miller?"

"You got it." Miller started unrolling the top of a paper bag he'd been carrying around.

"What's that?" I asked.

"You'll see." He kept unraveling the bag.

He'd brought it to the mall with him and kept it all scrunched up, so I'd figured it was something his mom was making him return, like one of his sister's skirts.

Instead of a skirt, Miller pulled out a t-shirt, unfurled it, and held it up to show the lettering on the front. *"He Swims Therefore He Drives."* After a moment, he tossed it to me. "It's yours. From me and Johnny B."

I held it out so I could read it again. "Clever. Thanks, guys. You shouldn't have."

"See, I told you we shouldn't have," Johnny B said to Miller. "Could have saved some cash."

"Shut up. He's just being polite. He loves it. Right, Nick?"

"Yeah, it's great. Nice to know you have confidence in me."

Johnny B snickered, and Miller rolled up the bag and held it behind his back.

"What?" I asked.

"Nothing. Nothing at all," Miller said, and Johnny B's snickering grew into full-fledged laughter.

"Go ahead, show him," Johnny B said, between guffaws.

Miller's face turned pink. "Forget it. Move along, move along, nothing to see here."

Johnny B took a quick step and grabbed the bag from Miller. He ripped it open and pulled out another t-shirt. With his long arms, he held it up, just beyond the reach of Miller's outstretched hands.

It read, *"Swimming Sucks. Driving Sucks. I'm a Biker."* Below the words was a picture of a teenager riding a tricycle.

"I take it back. You guys bite," I said.

"That's just a backup. In case…" Miller's face had turned almost purple.

"I told him it was a stupid idea," Johnny B said.

Obviously, they both thought they were being hilarious, and they wanted me to see both shirts, or they would have left one at home. I had to hand it to those guys, they did know how to cheer someone up.

Johnny B tossed me the other shirt, too. I rolled them up into a single roll and held it in my fist.

"So, you going to make it? Test is tomorrow, right?" Miller's face had returned to its normal pasty hue.

"I don't know. I think so."

"This is huge, you know. This could determine how your entire year goes. In fact, the rest of your high school experience hangs in the balance," Miller said, eyes wide.

"Dude..." Johnny B said out of the side of his mouth, intended for Miller's ears only.

"I mean, not being able to get your license? What will the girls think? Having your mom drive you around in the Bugmobile for dates? You might as well join a monastery."

Miller wasn't saying anything I hadn't thought myself, for just about every day of the summer. He was right about one thing: this was big. Huge. Luckily, the problem may have been identified. "Laura thinks it's all in my head."

Miller chimed in. "Well, she certainly knows a lot about he—"

I punched him in the shoulder. "Shut up. That's Laura you're talking about."

"Lighten up, dude." Miller rubbed his shoulder, glaring at me. "It was just a joke."

"Jokes are supposed to be funny." Johnny B slugged him in the other shoulder. He turned to me. "Go ahead, Nick."

"She says that I don't want to swim because I'm afraid to get my license. Because," I almost choked on the words, "...because a new driver killed my father in an auto accident."

Neither Johnny B nor Miller responded. None of us were used to dealing with raw emotions, unless you counted sarcasm as an emotion.

197

"She says that basically, my subconscious has been screwing me."

"At least you're getting some action," Miller mumbled under his breath.

Johnny B ignored him. "What do you think?"

"I don't know. Sounds plausible. I mean, the subconscious is real, right?"

"Abso-fucking-lutely," Miller said. "I think the subconscious is what drives us. It's the little guy working the joystick in your brain, controlling everything. That's why you should always be nice to him."

"I think the guy working your brain has been on an extended vacation," Johnny B said.

Miller flipped him off. "At least I've got a brain."

Johnny B faked a punch toward Miller's gut, then tapped him on the head with one of his long arms. Miller swatted it away and squared up in a fighter's stance.

"Cut it out, you clowns. I've got my freaking swimming test tomorrow. I need to concentrate."

"Too bad Allie won't be there for moral support, either," Miller said.

I'd told him about Allie going off to college. I'd conveniently omitted the rest of the embarrassing story, including my encounter with King Kong Harrison. I'd also somehow neglected to tell him of my swimming lesson with Laura.

"I'll be there," Johnny B said.

"Me too," Miller said.

"Well, with you guys there, how can I fail?" Laura said she'd be there, too. *That's* the kind of moral support that might actually help. I'd feel like a complete jackass if I flopped in front of her. "Anyone feel like a smoothie?"

"Who's buying?" Miller asked.

"I am."

"In that case, I feel like two," Miller said, ducking another left jab from Johnny B.

* * *

We closed down the mall, and Miller's father dropped me off at home. As soon as I opened the front door, I heard their voices, loud and sharp. My pulse quickened as I followed the racket to the kitchen.

Jason and my mom were standing, facing each other, about six feet apart. He was jabbing his finger at her as he yelled, and she was holding her ground, one hand on her hip, face crimson, also yelling. When they saw me, they both stopped and turned my way.

Jason spoke first. "Get lost. We're in the middle of something."

"Don't you speak to him like that," Mom said. "He can damn well stay."

Jason scowled at me, then at her.

Her eyes blazed. "Go ahead, big man. Keep talking. I'm sure Nick would love to hear what you did to his mother."

Jason licked his lips, and I could tell he was trying to figure out what to say next.

Mom turned to me. "Well, if he's too chicken to say anything, I will. Jason here was just denying that he has another girlfriend. He says the texts and calls on his phone were all a mistake. A wrong number." She laughed, without humor. "Oh, wait. That's what he said at first. When I pointed out that they were all from the same person, he claimed that they were from a former co-worker. When I *then* told him that some of the texts themselves were downright X-rated, he tried to get me to believe she was just a stalker." She turned back to Jason, who was standing there, wide-eyed. "How stupid do you think I am? Of course, I'm not surprised you didn't have the guts to tell me the truth that you wanted out of this relationship."

A vein in Mom's neck pulsed like crazy. I'd never seen her so mad, and that was saying something.

"What were you doing looking through my phone?" Jason asked.

Even I recognized his feeble attempt to put the blame back on Mom.

"It rang while you were in the shower. I was trying to do you a favor."

"Well, I don't need your favors. I don't need anything from you. You care more about those stupid bugs of yours than you do about me."

"They have more character, that's for sure. I can't believe how I fell for you and your shit." Mom inched forward, and I thought I noticed Jason flinch.

"The feeling is mutual. In fact, I don't know how your husband ever put up with you. You're a total bitch."

Mom moved closer to Jason and stuck her face up to his. "Asshole."

Jason started to raise his hand, as if he were winding up to slap Mom.

Before he could get his hand shoulder height, I lunged at him. Mom caught me with an arm around my waist, six inches before I made contact with Jason. She dug her heels in and tried to haul me back. I felt like tearing into Jason with my bare hands. My heart hammered. "You can't talk to my mom like that. And you can't talk about my dad, either!"

Jason's hands flew up in defense. "I don't hit little kids."

"Nick is not a little kid," she spat at Jason as she tightened her grip around my waist.

"Get out of here," I shouted. "Get out and leave us alone!" Tears began rolling down my cheeks. I clenched my fists, half hoping Jason would make the first move.

She put her mouth near my ear and spoke softly, so only I could hear. "Nick-o, don't do anything. Please. He's not worth it. Not by a long shot." I stopped struggling against Mom, and she walked me backward until we bumped into the wall.

I began to hyperventilate.

"Relax, Nick. Take a deep breath," Mom said.

I sucked in a lungful of air. Then another. Closed my eyes and let myself go slack.

"Thank you," she whispered.

I opened my eyes, turned my gaze over her shoulder at Jason.

Mom spun around. "Get the hell out of here."

"I'm gone. First thing in the morning," Jason said.

"You mean first thing right now." Mom's nostrils flared.

Jason stared at her for a couple of beats. Then he rushed from the room. A few seconds later, we heard his thundering footsteps up the stairs.

Mom left the kitchen and went straight to her favorite spot on the family room couch. I plopped down beside her and hugged her for the entire twenty-five minutes it took for Jason to pack up his stuff.

I didn't let go until the front door slammed, with Jason on the other side.

When it did, I hopped up and locked the deadbolt in case he tried to return. I got back to Mom to find her staring vacantly into space.

"Mom? You okay?" I settled down next to her, and she put her hand on my knee.

"I'll be okay. Just another bump in the road." She shook her head. "I guess I should have known. He wasn't the most mature guy I've ever dated. I just thought he'd change, you know, when he realized what was at stake. Am I such a bad catch?"

"Jason was a massive jerk," I said.

She offered a sad smile and a shrug. "Maybe. If that's true, then what does it say about me that I fell for him?"

"Sometimes it takes a while for a guy's jerkiness to emerge. You're better off without a guy who would do something like this. Seriously."

A few tears formed in Mom's eyes, and my cheeks also were wet. I couldn't remember the last time we'd had a cryfest.

"You are the best kid a mom could wish for. Don't ever change, okay?"

She leaned back while I fought away more tears. I cleared my throat and tried to sound as if I knew what I was talking about. "I'm sure you'll meet some other guy, one who's ten times better than Jason." *And one who isn't a cheating drug addict with a thing for weapons.*

"At least Gram will be relieved about all this. She certainly didn't like Jason, not one bit." She spoke through her tears. "And I guess you won't mind all that much, either."

"I don't know, Mom. It's just that...well, look what he did to you."

She wiped her eyes. "I love you, Nick-o. You're amazing, coming to my defense like that. Just like your father would have. He was the opposite of Jason. Kind and considerate, with an optimistic outlook. I called him Mr. Happy. No bad moods with that guy. You remind me a lot of him."

Clearly, Mom's perceptions were a bit hazy. She often got on my case about my moods.

"What bothers me most is that you didn't get to know him. He absolutely adored you."

I nodded. I'd seen baby pictures with my father carrying me on his shoulders, his face beaming. I always had a smile on my face, too.

"We went to high school together, you know."

I did know—Mom had told me some of this before, of course, but there was no way I was going to interrupt her. Not now. Hopefully, reminiscing about good times would take the sting out of what just happened.

"He was about your age now when I first met him. Isn't that a kick in the pants, to think you could already know who you're going to marry?"

I pictured Laura as she was, and I tried to picture her twenty years from now. That kinda weird, kinda good feeling swept through me again. I wonder if that's how Mom felt when she had been with my father.

"Our time together was wonderful. Too short, of course, and we had our share of disagreements, but somehow we always worked things out. We were totally, completely, in love." An edge grew in her voice. "And then one day, it was over. Compared to that, having Jason leave is a walk in the park on a beautiful afternoon. I hope that one day, Nick-o, you'll find someone as great as your father was to me. And I also hope you get to grow old together." She sniffled and wiped at her nose. Then, through a few more tears, she managed, "Now, you need to do me a giant favor. Forget about what just happened. You've got a big day tomorrow, and I'd feel terrible if this whole thing messed that up. So I want you to go to bed and get a good night's sleep. And dream buoyant thoughts!"

Chapter Twenty-Six: T-minus Zero

I Shoulda Moved to Iowa When I Had the Chance

I woke up while Mom was still asleep. After last night's events, I didn't think she'd be making it to my swim test, and I didn't blame her one bit. My friends would be there for moral support, and that was good enough for me.

I threw on my swim trunks, grabbed a pouch of Pop-Tarts, and left her a note on the kitchen table telling her I didn't need a ride, that I was going to take my bike and get there early. I needed a little quiet time to get myself psyched up—and to get my head straight after what happened. Every time I thought of the three of us, squaring off in the kitchen, I felt a surge of adrenaline.

Wearing a backpack stuffed with a change of clothes, towel, and goggles, I rode my bike down the familiar streets, coasting and taking it easy. My test wasn't until 9:00, so I had plenty of time to savor what I hoped was my last bike ride to the pool. As I got closer, worries about failing my test—and not getting my license—completely crowded out the thoughts of last night.

Though early, I already could feel the sun through my thin t-shirt, and breathing was like inhaling a sponge—a typically hot and humid late August day. Again, I pictured future excursions to the pool, when I'd be cruising in an air-conditioned Taurus. *My* air-conditioned Taurus.

All I had to do was swim the length of the pool and back, without touching bottom or grabbing onto the sides. No sweat.

Only a few cars were in the pool parking lot. The pool didn't officially open until 11:00; the cars probably belonged to the lifeguard running the test and the parents of the other kids hoping to prove they could swim.

I braked to a stop at the bike rack and locked my bike. Then, instead of heading inside, I circled around to the right, leaped over a ditch, and climbed a hill, giving me a clear view over the fence into the pool. I shrugged off my backpack and dumped it on the grass, then plopped down beside it. I unzipped the pocket and fished out my phone. Last night before bed, I loaded it with some inspirational music to get me pumped, just like the NBA players did before one of their match-ups.

I wedged the earbuds in and turned up the volume. *We Are the Champions* by Queen was first up. I gobbled down my Pop-Tarts, then I leaned back and listened to my playlist while I tried to convince myself I could swim.

The more I'd thought about what Laura had said, the more I bought into her theory. I didn't want to swim because I didn't want to kill anyone with my car. But that was faulty logic, for sure. Just because one newbie driver killed someone didn't mean *I* was going to kill someone. I laughed to myself. Putting it in those terms made my fear seem utterly, completely, undeniably ridiculous.

But there it was.

I prayed Laura was also right in her prognosis, that since I now knew what was holding me back, I could overcome it. She said I had all the physical aspects down pat. Just be calm, put everything together, and be one with the water. Oh yeah, swim like your life depended on it, too.

Across the parking lot, I spotted Johnny B and Miller ambling toward the pool. They wouldn't notice me unless I waved or yelled, so I leaned back and remained still. No way did I want to talk to them before the test. They wanted me to swim so badly that I was afraid they'd be so encouraging and patronizing I'd risk upchucking my Pop-Tarts.

I breathed a sigh of relief as they entered through the pool's front gate. I checked my phone. Still about fifteen minutes to go.

As the time approached, butterflies—big, honking butterflies—fluttered and flapped in my gut. *To be expected*, I told myself. *Just try to ignore them.*

While I worked on controlling my nerves, the Bugmobile drove up and zipped right into a space. Mom got out and hustled across the lot into the pool, and I felt the butterflies calm down, almost immediately. Why had I doubted her showing up? She was my mother, and she'd seen every stupid play and choir performance I'd ever been in throughout grade school. She would never miss something this important, no matter how bad she felt. I guessed the stress really was messing with my mind.

Even though I hated the guy, I felt bad about Jason leaving on one level, but deep down, I knew she was better off in the long run. Hopefully, she'd realize that before she expended too much emotional energy grieving about her loss. Now that he'd moved out, I considered—for the fiftieth time—telling her about the drugs and the gun, but she'd probably just think I was telling stories to make her feel better. So I decided to keep my mouth shut. Maybe when I was thirty and she'd been remarried for a while, I'd bring it up. Or not.

By the side of the pool, Johnny B and Miller sat next to each other; Mom walked by, said a few words to them, then took a seat two chairs away. She was always very polite to my friends, but I thought Miller frightened her in some way. He had that effect on a lot of people.

Ten minutes to go. I should report in to the lifeguard and warm up some. I'd gotten loose riding my bike, but I guessed it wouldn't hurt to stretch a little more. If nothing else, it might show the lifeguard I was serious about this swimming stuff.

I rose and hoisted my backpack onto my shoulders, then froze when I noticed Laura strolling down the sidewalk, approaching from the other direction. I wouldn't have minded talking to *her* before the test, but I'd run out of time, and besides, I was anxious enough. These days, talking to Laura was a fifty-fifty proposition—half the time I'd get less nervous, half the time I'd get more nervous. Go figure.

Her words came back to me. *You're a good driver and you're a good swimmer.* Right now, I'd settle for *barely competent.*

I waited until she went in before I jogged down the hill. I passed through the men's locker room and out onto the pool deck. I allowed myself a quick glance and a small wave to my group of fans. Mom called out, "Yoo hoo, Nick-o. Go get 'em, tiger."

I looked the other way and pretended I didn't hear.

Time to get down to business. I searched for the lifeguard conducting the test, but didn't see one. There were three other kids—all much younger—waiting by the lap lanes at the shallow end of the pool, so I wandered over.

"Uh, are you here for the swimming test?" I asked the tallest one, who didn't quite come up to my chest. He was maybe ten years old.

"Yeah." He gave me the stink-eye for a moment, then jerked his thumb at the others, a boy and a girl, both around six or seven years old. "Them too. Why?"

"That's what I'm here for."

He looked me up and down with a sneer on his munchkin face. "Really?"

"Yeah, really." I put some attitude in it. "Where's the lifeguard running the show?"

"I wish. The Pool Czar is doing the test. She's mean, you know."

Oh shit, did I know. "Don't worry, you'll do fine," I said, trying to put him at ease. I knew how I felt, and I was six or seven years older than he was.

"Oh, I'm not worried. She's not mean to me." He snapped his goggles into place. "Well...good luck, dude." He stepped away, swinging his arms like Michael Phelps does before winning a gold medal.

The butterflies that had been swarming in my stomach gave way to blackbirds. PZ was giving the test? I'd figured it would be one of the lifeguards who might show me some pity for being one of their peers or for trying so hard or just because they didn't want to wreck a kid's life for not swimming. But PZ? She'd be like a shark in the water waiting for the first piece of chum—or the first chump—to appear. Two gobbles later, it would be over.

Gulp.

The clock on the wall above the pool office read nine o'clock, straight up. On cue, PZ emerged from the office wearing a whistle around her neck and a scowl on her face.

Double gulp.

She shuffled in our direction, scowl unwavering. The other kids gathered into a clump and took up a position behind me. PZ stopped and placed her hands on her hips. "Good morning, swimmers. You all are here for swimming test, no?"

I sensed three heads bobbing behind me, but not a sound. I'd been elected group mouthpiece when I wasn't looking. "Uh, yes, that's right."

She glared at me, then consulted a clipboard she clutched in one skeletal hand. "Mary Atkins? Todd Atkins? Ryan Keever?"

Three small voices said "yes" simultaneously.

PZ tapped her clipboard, but didn't call my name.

"Uh, I'm Nick Carlin." I shifted my weight from one foot to the other.

"Yes, I know who you are." PZ's glare intensified. She addressed the group. "You have three minutes to warm up in pool. Then we start with Ryan Keever. Then Nick Carlin. Then Atkins girl. Then Atkins boy." She blew the whistle around her neck. "Begin."

The three little kids flung themselves into the pool as if a race had begun. I followed them in and shivered at the shock of the cold water, just like I shivered every single stupid time I jumped into the pool. Some people just weren't comfortable in the water, and I was one of them. I grumbled to myself for a moment, then remembered I needed a positive attitude. *Be one with the water. Stay calm, stay focused.* I stopped shivering and ducked my head underwater to wet my hair.

Before I knew it, the three minutes were up, and PZ was tooting her whistle again. "Okay. Out of pool. We begin test now."

We hauled ourselves out of the water and stood dripping in front of PZ. Behind her, on the other side of the pool, my cheering section looked on, although if I didn't know better, I'd say Miller was checking out someone's mother sitting in front of him. Laura was staring in my direction, hands clasped together as if she were praying. Smart girl. My mother waved when she saw me glance in her direction. I quickly returned my attention to PZ before I came completely unglued.

"To pass test, you swim across pool to deep end, touch wall and swim back here and touch wall. You must not touch bottom and you must not touch side. And no hanging on lane markers or wall." She looked at each of us individually to see if we were paying attention. I didn't know about the rest, but I sure was.

PZ grabbed the stopwatch that hung around her neck with the whistle and held it up in the air. "You have two minutes to complete lap. Any questions?"

WTF?

The bottom fell out of my stomach. Two minutes? Since when was this a timed test? "Uh, excuse me. I didn't know we had a time limit. No one ever mentioned that. There must be some mistake."

"No mistake," she said, with what I was sure was a small smile. On her, it was terrifying. She stepped closer and rotated the face of the stopwatch toward me. Moved it six inches in front of my nose. Tapped the glass with a yellowed fingernail. "You have two minutes. If you can swim, it is not problem. If you cannot swim, then you cannot swim. All the time in world cannot help you." Something flickered in her eyes. Was she enjoying this? Was this her way of getting payback for all the horsing around she thought I was guilty of?

In case of disaster—if I had to catch my breath, or got cramps, or whatever—I'd planned to float on my back or dogpaddle until I recovered. I figured I had time, and technically it complied with the no-touching rules. Now, I was screwed. With the time limit, I'd have to swim straight through, cramps be damned. I glanced again at Mom, wondering what she would do if I went over and told her PZ was being mean to me. If I were five years old, she'd hug me and whisper that she'd take care of things. Now...

I was on my own. Growing up was a bitch.

PZ ran a bony finger along her clipboard. "Okay. Mr. Keever. Please take your mark."

Ryan walked to the edge of the pool, then inched forward until his toes curled around the concrete lip. He crouched and stuck his arms behind him, ready to throw them forward as he dove in.

"On your mark. Get set. Go." She blew the whistle, and little Ryan Keever launched himself into the pool. After some sleek underwater gliding, he surfaced and started swimming. Nice smooth strokes, furious kicking, confident breathing. This ten-year-old could swim.

I took mental notes and visualized swimming like little Ryan Keever.

He moved through the water like an otter. When he reached the far side, he executed some kind of fancy underwater, flipping, acrobatic turn and headed back our way, now a torpedo homing in on its target. I glanced at PZ and noticed admiration on her face. Maybe those good feelings would last a little longer.

Across the pool, people clapped and cheered as Ryan approached the finish line. A lady, his mother no doubt, came rushing over to greet him as he finished.

Ryan touched the wall, and PZ made a big show of stopping her timer. Ryan hung on to the wall, gazing up at PZ with a broad smile on his face. "Congratulations, Mr. Keever. You passed in one minute, nine seconds. Very well done."

Ryan punched the air a couple times, then slapped the water in celebration. He yanked off his goggles, tossed them onto the pool deck, and climbed out. As he passed me, he held his fist out and I bumped it. Then his mother swooped in and draped a SpongeBob towel around his shoulders and hugged him, all the while telling him how great he did.

I was pretty sure Mom had left my SpongeBob towel at home.

I tried to get a read from Ryan's swim. He'd been moving pretty good, but he was only ten. I was bigger and stronger. If he finished in just over one minute, that gave me some hope. I could swim almost a minute slower and still pass.

I wasn't proud either. I'd take a 1:59:59 without thinking twice. I'd even fist bump PZ.

"Mr. Carlin. Please take your mark."

I pulled the goggles down from my forehead and worked them into place, making sure the seal was tight, and I could see okay. I flapped my arms and shook my legs out, one at a time. Then I managed to gulp down a few deep breaths, purposely not glancing at Mom or my friends. I had enough pressure on me.

PZ removed the whistle from her mouth. "Mr. Carlin. We are waiting. Please take your mark." She stuffed the whistle back in, and pointed the stopwatch at me, finger twitching on the button.

Two giant steps took me to the pool edge. I mimicked Ryan and curled my toes over the lip and crouched, ready to explode. Slowly, I extended my arms behind me and concentrated on a spot in the water about two meters out. I gave a quick nod, just to signal PZ I was ready, knowing full well she'd blow the whistle when she damn well pleased, ready or not.

The shrill tweet still startled me.

I sprang forward and threw my arms out, bringing my hands together way above my head. For an instant, I was flying through the air, then I hit the water, my belly slapping the surface in a semi-belly flop. I hadn't practiced my starting dives very much.

Smarting, I tried to put the poor start out of my mind and focus on the stroke. Extend and pull with the right hand, then extend and pull with the left. I had two strokes under my belt when I remembered I needed to kick. I started kicking furiously and felt myself moving through the water. Swimming.

Stroke, stroke, stroke. The moment of truth was fast approaching— my first breath. I waited until just after my right arm cleared, then I turned my head out of the water, opened my mouth and sucked in some air. I braced for the inevitable rush of pool water, but none came. I closed my mouth quickly and turned my head back into the water.

I did it. I'd breathed. I resisted the temptation to laugh, I felt so relieved. I actually breathed properly! If I could do that a dozen more times, I was home free.

Bolstered by my achievement, I worked on maintaining a steady rhythm. Stroke, stroke. Kick, kick, kick, kick. I tried to banish everything else from my mind, but I could hear the cheering from my fans. I couldn't make out what they were saying, just a bunch of excited noise.

Breath number two came easily. What had all the fuss been about? Swimming was a piece of cake.

I maintained the pace, envisioning myself behind the wheel of my Taurus, Laura in the passenger seat, gazing at me with puppy eyes. I kept stroking and kicking, stroking and kicking.

I'd been cruising along and didn't want to bonk into the wall, so I lifted my head out of the water to see where I was. I was barely halfway across! My heart sank, and I prayed the rest of me wouldn't follow.

Gritting my teeth, I stroked harder. I'd never really swum this far before, so I didn't have any idea about my speed. I had to be going at least as fast as that munchkin Ryan, didn't I? The thought of some puny fifth-grader beating me out spurred me on.

I kicked with as much ferocity as I could while I pulled myself through the water. I tried to muster every ounce of energy I had and applied it to my arms and legs. In a couple of minutes this would be all over; I could rest for a month. I had to succeed, knowing my life as an independent—and mobile—high school student depended on it.

It didn't take long at this furious pace for the muscles in my quads to begin shrieking. They were followed almost immediately by a wail from my left calf. My body was protesting the stressful exertion—loudly.

I was so preoccupied by the pain in my legs that I forgot to breathe in rhythm. I hurried through a stroke and gasped for air before my mouth had fully cleared the surface. Water gushed in, and I sputtered, spitting it out and gasping for air at the same time. My arms stopped stroking smoothly and slapped at the water. My kicking waned to a few feeble flutters.

Panic seized me. I wasn't worried about drowning anymore. And it wasn't so much the fear of failing the test that bothered me. It was looking like a loser in front of Laura. I tried to pull it all together. Took a few dog paddles to get myself righted. Gulped in some air and willed myself to continue.

Then time seemed to pause, and a million thoughts swirled in my brain. About swimming and driving, about Mom and Jason, about my father and the kid who killed him, high as a kite. Visions of Laura and Miller, of Allie Merskie, and Emily, the girl from the lake, all danced in my mind. Guns, drugs, Herb in his black socks and boxers. Everything that had me mega-stressed all summer came bubbling up, like a backed-up sewer drain. My synapses fired randomly, and I saw colors and shapes and happiness and sorrow.

All while I took a few dog paddles at the neighborhood pool.

In an instant, the chaos in my head passed, and my mission crystallized once again. I needed to get my ass to the wall, then back across the pool as quickly as possible—I'd wasted some time treading water.

Failing was not an option.

I stuck my head back into the water and started swimming. Arms and legs in sync, ignoring the pain. In the background, the cheering and yelling seemed to intensify, and I channeled that energy into my effort.

And most importantly, I didn't forget to breathe.

Ten strokes later, I approached the far wall. I timed my turn as best I could, and although it wasn't a fancy one like Ryan had executed, it did the job. I headed back toward the finish line.

My heart pumped faster than I could ever remember. My legs churned a white wake behind me. My arms were like vanes of a windmill, moving in rhythm and propelling my body through the pool. I was becoming one with the water, and Laura had been right. It felt great. I was in the zone. It may have taken me years and years to learn how to swim, but I'd done it.

Fifteen meters to go, and I could feel the laminated driver's license in my hand. Then I heard the harsh sound of a whistle. People shouting. More noise. Yelling. More whistles. I ignored the cacophony and swam as fast as I could.

I felt a *thwap* on my shoulder, then another *thwap* on my skull. I turned my head, and the end of a neon orange Styrofoam pool noodle slapped the water three inches from my face. PZ was pacing me on the pool deck, blowing her whistle and hitting me with a noodle.

I guessed my two minutes were up.

I didn't care. I veered to my left toward the middle of the pool, away from the crazy Pool Czar. On the opposite side of the deck, I noticed a few people had gotten out of their chairs and were standing by the edge, screaming at me, encouraging me, inspiring me. A chant began, "Nick, Nick, Nick."

I swam faster. The whistle had stopped, and all I heard were my well-wishers, exhorting me to finish.

I did, and when my hand hit the wall, I sprang up, flung my goggles off, and hurled them back into the pool. My cheering section applauded. Unfortunately, my victory was short-lived. PZ came scurrying over and bent down to talk to me.

"You did not pass, Mr. Carlin. You exceeded two minutes. I am sorry." Her smile belied her words. *Sorry, my ass.* "Now. Please exit pool. I have more swimmers for test." She turned on her heels and stalked off to torture the Atkins siblings.

I slogged over to the stairs in the corner of the pool, and climbed out, legs like lead weights. My friends gathered off to one side, not quite sure how to behave. One minute, I was about to conquer Everest, the next minute I was tumbling down the mountain, covered in snow. Mom came rushing up first.

"You did it, Nick-o. You swam." Her face had turned red, and I detected a tear or two at the corners of her eyes.

"I failed, Mom."

She took my chin in her hand, gave it a squeeze. "No, you didn't. Not in the least. I don't care how long it takes you to swim, just that you make it. It could have taken you an hour, and I wouldn't care. You passed, Nick-o. With flying colors. Don't think I haven't noticed how hard you've been working. And hard work usually pays off. I'm proud of you, Nick-o. Not just for working hard, but for everything. For being my best guy." Now her tears began to flow a little stronger.

I felt my own gusher getting ready to burst forth, so I moved on, making sure I understood what she was saying. "So, I can get my license?"

"Sure, honey. As long as you pass all the driving tests, of course."

"Thanks. It feels..." I stopped talking and cleared my throat, afraid to continue. If I did, I knew I'd end up choking on my words.

Mom held my gaze, and her face slowly brightened, followed by a smile. The happy smile, not the wistful one. "You must be relieved."

"Yeah. That's a good word for it." I glanced over her shoulder at Miller, Johnny B, and Laura. They huddled together whispering, no doubt plotting ways to console me. Either that, or they were working up schedules for chauffeuring me around the next few years.

I nodded at my friends. "Can I tell them the good news?"

Mom stepped back. "Sure. I need to get to work anyway—another urgent situation. How about a celebration dinner tonight? At Frankie's? I'll see if Gram can join us."

"Do you feel up to it?" I asked.

She put her hand on my shoulder. "Life goes on. I'll be fine. In fact, helping you celebrate will be good for me."

"Then, sure. Let's do it." I spotted Laura peeking over her shoulder at me. "Can I bring a friend?"

"Okay by me." She tapped her watch. "Sorry, but I got some bugs to kill." Mom winked at me, waved goodbye to my friends from a distance, and headed off toward the exit. She slowed and made a face at me as she passed behind PZ, who was finishing up the swimming tests.

Miller must have drawn the short straw, because he came over first, while the other two watched. He approached slowly, as if I might attack him in a rage of defeat. "Hey. Good swim."

"Thanks." I didn't smile or anything, never passing up a chance to yank Miller's chain. "I didn't make it in under two minutes, though. I failed the test."

He nodded somberly. "Well, you can always try again next year, right?"

I shook my head. "No, I don't think I'll be trying again."

"What?" Miller's eyes grew to Frisbee size. "But if you don't pass the test, your mom—"

I held my hand up. "It's cool. She said I can get my license. I proved I could swim, and that's all she cared about."

Miller exhaled with such force I was surprised he didn't bring up a few whitecaps on the pool's surface. "Man, that's awesome." He turned and called to the others. "Coast is clear. He passed!"

Johnny B and Laura rushed over, offering their congratulations. Seems everyone was relieved. I hadn't realized how much they'd been pulling for me. "Thanks, guys. And thanks for cheering me on during the test."

"I wanted to smack the Pool Czar with a noodle myself," Johnny B said. "What a witch."

"You did great, Nick. Just great," Laura said.

"Yeah, great, Nick. Just great," Miller said, mocking Laura in a sing-song falsetto.

Laura laughed and Johnny B jabbed Miller in the shoulder, then started chasing him around the pool deck, trying to swat him. Luckily for them, the swimming tests had ended, and PZ had disappeared back into her cave.

"You really did do great." Laura stepped closer.

"Well, I owe it to you. You figured it all out."

She shook her head. "You already knew how to swim. I just made a few tweaks."

"I'm not talking about at the pool. I'm talking about what you said to me at the pond. All that psychological stuff. That was the key." I tapped the side of my head. "You get me. You always have."

She smiled and glanced away at the ground. When she picked her head up, there was something else in her eyes. Something I'd only dreamed about. "So…"

"So…" I reached out and took her hand. "So."

She stretched up on her toes and kissed me on the cheek. "So there."

"I guess we'll see what happens, won't we?"

"Yeah. As long as it doesn't screw up our friendship. Deal?"

"Deal." I shook her hand. "Hey, do you want to go to dinner tonight, with my mom and grandmother?"

"Like a date?"

"Exactly like a date."

"Sure. I'd like that."

"Outstanding," I said. "Can I call you later? Right now, I want to go tell Gram I passed. And take another look at my new ride." I pointed at Johnny B and Miller, who were off in the grassy area behind the pool deck, wrestling on the ground. "Tell those two I had to leave, will you?"

"Forget them. They'll figure it out on their own." Laura said goodbye, then gave me another kiss on the cheek.

I left the pool and hopped on my bike. If I were any more pumped up, I wouldn't even need to ride over to Gram's, I'd be able to float on the breeze. As I pedaled, the muscles in my legs ached, reminding me of my swim. I did it. I'd passed the swimming test. All my hard work had paid off.

And Laura and I had moved on to the next level. It had been quite a day, and it wasn't yet noon.

I turned the corner of Gram's street and noticed flashing red lights. An ambulance and a police car were parked in front of her house. Across the street, a small cluster of neighbors watched the commotion.

I pumped my legs as fast as I could, then skidded to a stop, jumped off my bike, and dumped it on the curb.

CHAPTER TWENTY-SIX: T-MINUS ZERO

I raced to her house as fast as my feet would take me.

Acknowledgments

I may have written the words, but so many others helped shape those words into a story and then into an actual book.

My sincerest thanks go to:

The great folks (and good friends) at Level Best Books: my editor extraordinaire Verena Rose, uber-talented cover designer Shawn Reilly Simmons, and the super-efficient Deb Well.

The many readers and critique partners I've worked with through the years: Dan Phythyon and Ayesha Court. Dorothy Patton. Mark Skehan. Doug Bell. John Stevenson, Jill Balboni, Kim Stevenson, and Samantha Stevenson. Andy Heyman, Todd Hall. Lorraine Storms. Fred Rexroad. Tara Laskowski. Barb Goffman. John Betancourt, Carla Coupe, Bonner Menking, Adam Meyer, Megan Plyler. Ed Aymar. Eric Smith. Sangu Mandanna, Lizzie Cooke, and Erica Cameron.

The Rumpi: Donna Andrews, Ellen Crosby, John Gilstrap, and Art Taylor. Amazing writers and friends.

My awesome crime fiction community: Mystery Writers of America, International Thriller Writers, and Sisters in Crime. My pals throughout cyberspace.

The P.J. Parrish sisters (Kris Montee and Kelly Nichols), Reed Farrel Coleman, Elaine Raco Chase, Jeff Deaver, Jim Grady, Hank Phillippi Ryan, Lori Rader-Day, Eli Cranor. Supportive teachers, mentors, and blurbers!

My (numerous) extremely patient swimming instructors.

Booksellers, librarians, and, of course, my faithful readers.

My terrific, terrific agent, Michelle Richter, and the entire group at Fuse Literary.

My extended family.

My parents, for everything.

My children, Mark and Stuart, and my wife, Janet. My inspirations—in fiction and in life.

Thanks everyone!

About the Author

Alan Orloff has published twelve novels and more than sixty short stories. His work has won an Anthony, an Agatha, a Derringer, and two ITW Thriller Awards. He's also been a finalist for the Shamus Award and has had a story selected for THE BEST AMERICAN MYSTERY STORIES anthology. He loves cake and arugula, but not together. Never together. He lives and writes in South Florida, where the examples of hijinks are endless. www.alanorloff.com

AUTHOR WEBSITE
  https://alanorloff.com/

SOCIAL MEDIA HANDLES:
  https://www.facebook.com/alanorloff
  https://bsky.app/profile/alanorloff.bsky.social
  https://www.threads.net/@alanorloff

https://www.instagram.com/alanorloff/

Also by Alan Orloff

Novels

Diamonds for the Dead, Midnight Ink, 2010 (Agatha Award Finalist)

Killer Routine, Midnight Ink, 2011

Deadly Campaign, Midnight Ink, 2012

The Taste, 2011

First Time Killer, 2012

Ride-Along, 2013

Running From the Past, Kindle Press/Amazon Publishing, 2015

Pray for the Innocent, Kindle Press/Amazon Publishing, 2018 (ITW Thriller Award Winner)

I Know Where You Sleep, Down & Out Books, February 2020 (Shamus Award Finalist)

I Play One On TV, Down & Out Books, July 2021 (Agatha Award Winner, Anthony Award Winner)

Sanctuary Motel, Level Best Books, October 2023

Late Checkout, Level Best Books, October 2024 (Anthony Award

Finalist)

Hollywood Kills (anthology), co-editor, Level Best Books, July 2025

Short Stories *(60+ including one in five consecutive* Best New England Crime Stories *anthologies)*

Notable ones:

"Rule Number One" appeared in *Snowbound* and was selected for Best American Mystery Stories 2018.

"Dying in Dokesville" appeared in Malice Presents: *Mystery Most Geographical* and won a Derringer Award.

"Rent Due" appeared in *Mickey Finn: 21st Century Noir*, Vol. 1 and won an ITW Thriller Award